wide
awake
now

Also by David Levithan

wide awake now

david levithan

Alfred A. Knopf
New York

To everyone who supports LGBTQIA+ rights,
LGBTQIA+ literature, and LGBTQIA+ people

PART ONE

one

"I can't believe there's going to be a gay Jewish president."

As my mother said this, she looked at my father, who was still staring at the screen. They were shocked, barely comprehending.

Me?

I sat there and beamed.

two

I think it was the Jesus Freaks who were the happiest the next day at school. Most of the morning papers were saying that Stein's victory wouldn't have been possible without the Jesus Revolution, and I don't think Mandy or Janna or any of the other members of The God Squad would've argued. Mandy was wearing their JESUS IS LOVE T-shirt, while Janna had a LOVE THY NEIGHBOR button on her bag, right above the STEIN FOR PRESIDENT sticker. When they saw me walk through the door, they cheered and ran over, bouncing me into a jubilant hug. I wasn't the only gay Jew they knew, but I was the one they knew best, and we'd all been volunteers on the Stein/Martinez campaign together. After the hugging was done, we stood there for a moment and looked at one another with utter astonishment. We'd done it. Even though we wouldn't be able to vote for another two years, we'd helped to make this a reality. It was the most amazing feeling in the world, to know that something right had happened, and to know that it had happened not through luck or command but simply because enough people had understood it was right.

Some of our fellow students walked by us and smiled. Others scoffed or scowled—there were plenty of people in our school who would've been happy to shove our celebration into a locker and keep it there for four years.

"It was only by one state," one of them grunted. "Only seventy-six thousand votes in Kansas."

"Yeah, but who got the popular vote?" Mandy challenged.

The guy just spat on the ground and moved on.

"Did he really just spit?" Janna asked. "Ew."

I was looking everywhere for Jimmy. As soon as the results had been announced, I'd gone to my room to call him.

"Can you believe it?" I'd asked.

"I am so so so happy," he'd answered.

And I was so so so happy, too. Not only because of the election but because Jimmy was around to share it with. I had two things to believe in now, and in a way they felt related. After years of questioning whether the world was only going to get worse, I believed in the future, and in our future.

"I love you," he'd said at the end of the call, his voice bleary from the hour but sweetened by the news.

"I love you, too," I'd replied. "Good night."

"A very good night."

Now I wanted the continuation, the kiss that would seal

it. Stein had triumphed, the electoral college was secure, and I was in love with a boy who was in love with me.

"Somewhere Jesus is smiling," Janna said.

"Praise be," Mandy chimed in.

Keisha and Mira joined us in the halls, fingers entwined. They looked beamy, too.

"Not a bad day for gay Jew boys, huh?" Keisha said to me.

"Not a bad day for Afro-Chinese lesbians, either," I pointed out.

Keisha nodded. "You know it's the truth."

We had all skipped school the previous two days to get out the vote. Since most of us weren't old enough to drive, we acted as dispatchers, fielding calls from Kennedy-conscious old-age-home residents and angry-enough agoraphobic liberals, making sure the buses came to take them to the polls. Other kids, like Jimmy, had been at the polling places themselves, getting water and food for people as they waited hours for their turn to vote. (Our state hadn't made it illegal to give people water and food, like some other states.)

I felt that history was happening. Not like a natural disaster or New Year's Eve. No, this was human-made history, and here I was, an infinitesimally small part of it. We all were.

Suddenly I felt two arms wrap around me from behind, the two palms coming to rest at the center of my chest. Two very familiar hands—the chewed-up fingernails, the dark skin a little darker at the knuckles, the wire-thin pinkie ring, the bright red watch. The bracelet with two beads on it, jade for him and agate for me. I wore one just like it.

I smiled then—the same way I smiled every time I saw Jimmy. Part of my happiness lived wherever he was.

"Beautiful day," he said to me.

"Beautiful day," I agreed, then turned in his arms to sanctify the morning with our *this is real* kiss.

The first bell rang. I still had to run to my locker before homeroom.

"Everything feels a little different today, doesn't it?" Jimmy asked. We kissed again, then parted. But his words echoed with me. I was too young to remember when the Supreme Court upheld the rights of gay Americans, and all the weddings started happening. But I imagined that day felt a lot like today. I'd heard so many older people talk about it, about what it meant to know you had the same right as everyone else. I wasn't alive when Obama was elected, either, and instead came to consciousness at a time when there was a bigot on the megaphone, dividing the country further and shoving us right into a pandemic. I spent sixth grade at home, barely learning and never seeing my friends. Even when the bigot with the megaphone lost his election, things didn't get much better. We were still in a pandemic. People yelled at each other more and more, in no small part because they could yell from their bedrooms instead of having to actually leave the house to do it face to face. This past election was absolutely brutal. But the brutality of it was an issue itself, and I think finally enough people were like, *This is not how we should be.* Enough of us believed we had to unplug the hate machine before it destroyed us all.

I understood that now that Stein had won, he was likely to become more moderate to get along with Congress, especially since we'd only won by the margin of Kansas. But still . . . everything *did* feel a little different. Yes, the kids walking the halls around me were the same kids who'd been there yesterday. The books in my locker were piled just the way I'd left them. Mr. Farnsworth, my homeroom teacher, waited impatiently by his door, just like he always did. But it was like someone had upped the wattage of all the lights by a dozen watts. Someone had made the air two shades easier to breathe.

I knew this feeling wouldn't last. As soon as I realized it was euphoria, I knew it couldn't last. I couldn't even hold on to it. I could only ride within it as far as it would carry me.

The second bell rang. I sprinted into class, and Mr. Farnsworth closed the door.

"I expect to see you standing today," he said to me.

This was the deal we had: If Stein won the Presidency, I would stand for the Pledge of Allegiance for the first time since elementary school. Even back then, I hated the way it seemed to be something rote and indoctrinated—most people saying the words emptily, without understanding them. To me, the whole notion that we had to pledge allegiance seemed antithetical to the notion of freedom of speech. Mr. Farnsworth told me that the whole "project of

America" was about navigating seeming contradictions—in this case, finding a way to show allegiance to the idea of freedom without it imposing on that freedom.

"It's called a pledge," he said, "but the most important part is that nobody's keeping track of who pledges and who doesn't. It's American to recite it, but it's also crucially American for it to be voluntary."

Even when I wasn't making the whole pledge, I'd always said the six last words, because they were the ones I believe in, more than the concept of indivisibility. Today I said them extra loud, standing up.

With liberty and justice for all.

When I went to sit down, I found that my chair wasn't there. I landed butt-first on the floor.

"What's the matter, Duncan?" Jesse Marin's voice taunted. "Forgot where you belong?"

There was some laughter, but most of it was Jesse's. He cracked himself up on a regular basis.

He clearly hadn't interpreted the election as an unplugging of the hate machine. Because for some people, the hate machine was like a fossil fuel—they couldn't imagine having any power without it.

"That's how it goes," Jesse went on. "You stand up for something, you end up falling down on your ass."

Jesse's parents were big Decents in our town, and like most Decents he wasn't taking defeat very well. You would've thought he'd be used to it now, with all the changes that had happened as the pandemic recovery began. With each step away from hate and division, the Decents had sworn it meant the demise of civilization. But, of course, civilization did okay without the Decents proclaiming what needed to be censored and who needed to be "protected." They'd been smart at first—labeling everyone who wasn't a Decent as indecent. The initial reaction to that was to say "No, I'm not indecent!" or "What I'm doing is not indecent!"—which immediately put us on the defensive. It was only when we could say "Actually, I'm decent and you have no right to call me otherwise" that changes began.

Love is more decent than hate.

Community is more decent than conflict.

Kindness is more decent than violence.

These were our tenets. This was our pushback. They tried to bind our rights with unsupportable laws. They tried to stoke fear of trans people and people of color, hoping to energize the declining white, cis minority. They tried to alienate parents from the educational system so they could impose their own system and educate people to be like them and depend on their products. They tried to garble the voting process as much as they could, thinking we'd shy away, that we'd be lazy when our lives were at stake. We fought in order to stop fighting. We got, tenuously, to the bare minimum of where we needed to be.

The Decents didn't even call themselves "the Decents" anymore. We'd won back the word, just as we'd won back words like *moral* and *right* and *compassionate*. Because words mattered. Winning the words was a good part of the battle. And we won them by defining them correctly.

The principal's voice came over the speakers and read the morning announcements. He made no mention of the election; to him, the only part of the future worth noting was the Conservation Club's bake sale next Thursday and the football team's game against Voorhees on Saturday. *School is its own country,* he seemed to be saying in all that he wasn't saying. *I am the leader here, and I am not subject to any election. What happens in the world at large remains at large while you are here.*

I wanted to say something back to Jesse, to gloat or to cut him down. But then I thought of what Janna and Mandy would do, and I decided that I couldn't let winning make me any less kind.

I could see Mr. Farnsworth keeping watch over me, wondering what I was going to do. When the bell rang, I made eye contact with him and received a small, approving nod. Then, as I was about to pass by his desk, he asked me to stay back for a second.

Once the other students had gone, he said, "If I'm not mistaken, you're in Mr. Davis's first-period class."

I nodded.

"Look, Duncan, be careful today. He's not taking this well. He wants to detonate on someone—don't let it be you."

I looked at Mr. Farnsworth. I knew nothing about his

life—where he lived, how he voted, who he loved. But I could see he was genuinely worried. For me, yes. But for something bigger, too.

"I'll be careful," I promised.

And then I headed to Mr. Davis's class.

three

The plus about Mr. Davis's class: Jimmy was in it.

The minus: Mr. Davis was in it, too.

Both Jimmy and I had tried to switch out, but it was the only history class available first period. At the start, in September, Mr. Davis had been bad enough—he still held on to the idea that, say, the Indigenous population got a great deal when the Pilgrims came over, and that the word *savage* was acceptable to use in a history class, as if killing someone with an arrow was somehow more horrible than doing it with a gun or a bomb. Jimmy and I figured we could get through it because other teachers had already told us the truth, not just the Thanksgiving version. But then, as the election heated up, Mr. Davis seemed to forget he was teaching history and started lecturing us on current events instead. At one point, he let it slip to our class that he was an Iraq War Re-enactor, which disturbed me so much that

I went to my guidance counselor and complained. I'd read in magazines about what Iraq War Re-enactors did—the "interrogations," the simulated rescues, the ill-equipped soldiers facing ambushes, the falsified evidence—and I didn't want to have anything to do with a teacher involved in such things. My guidance counselor understood, but explained about needing the history class and promised she would have a talk with Mr. Davis about not making inappropriate statements. This was, of course, the last thing I wanted her to do—but she did it anyway, and soon Mr. Davis was railing into "the Steinheads" even more.

To Mr. Davis, the three worst things that had ever happened were:

1) The Jesus Revolution
2) Stein's candidacy
3) The concept of equality

because

1) Saying Jesus would be kind and loving instead of vengeful and violent didn't fit into Mr. Davis's plans.

2) Two words: Gay. Jewish. Although he'd never say it in only two words.

3) Every time another group became equal to straight cis white guys, it made Mr. Davis feel like he had that much less power . . . when the truth was that he never should've had so much power in the first place.

In choosing the three worst things that had ever happened, he conveniently forgot (among other things) the fundamental fact that our country was built on brutally stolen land using brutally stolen labor, and that this fact would never be justifiable. Like most countries, America was good at substituting mythology when history was inconvenient. Mr. Davis preferred to be a mythology teacher.

I hadn't been looking forward to Mr. Davis's class on that postelection morning; Mr. Farnsworth's warning only made me more nervous. I would've skipped it—and I'm sure Jimmy would've joined me—if I hadn't been certain that Mr. Davis would use it as an excuse to fail us. I wanted to pass Mr. Farnsworth's warning on to Jimmy, but I was late to class, and Mr. Davis had seated us as far away from each other as possible, as if we might overpower the room with gayness if we weren't separated by three rows of chairs. The joke was that he put me between Keisha and Mira instead. I told them to lay low once Mr. Davis came into the room; Keisha tried to spread the word, but Mr. Davis barged in at that moment and slammed the door so hard the map of the world shook.

I hoped Jimmy would avoid poking the bear.

He didn't look afraid. But then, Jimmy never looked afraid. The first time we ever went out, I was so nervous my leg shook. But Jimmy could have been napping, for all the insecurity he showed. Not that he seemed sleepy; the thing I recognized right away was that he was paying attention to me—not just to the things I was saying, but to details I didn't even know I was giving him.

It was, of all things, a homework date, made so casually that I wasn't even sure it was a date until he was kissing me. At the end of school one day last year, he'd asked me to come over to work on physics together. Giddy and terrified, I'd said yes, then ran to get my books before either of us could change our minds. As we walked home, I kept drying my palms in my pockets, while he talked about why he was sure physics was going to end up as his worst subject. When we got to his house, he offered me some pretzels and settled us down in his living room, where a muted screen was tuned to a news channel.

At first, we stuck to the subject. *How much weight needs to be attached to pulley x to get weight y up incline z?* But then, with a smile, he started to weave other questions in. *If the weight of y is doubled and the incline of z is halved, do you feel you're more an optimist or a pessimist? If we add two more weights, w1 and w2, to pulley x, would you mind if I told you that you have beautiful eyes?*

I thought there was no way my eyes could be as beautiful as his. I looked at them, shy, then looked a little lower and saw a gentle scattering of freckles across the top of his cheeks.

"You have freckles," I said.

"Probably my Irish great-grandfather . . . but who knows? When you have African and Indian and Irish and French and Catalan grandparents and great-grandparents—well, it's all just a mix."

I wanted to tell him it was a wonderful mix, but I was

afraid of sounding corny. We sat there on the floor for a moment, our problem sets spread out like kindergarten drawings between us. I had liked him for so long without being able to say it. Now here we were, the pulleys and the weights and the inclinations moving into their delicate balance, that equilibrium of desire, awaiting the conversion of thoughts and feelings into words and movements.

My leg shook. He reached over and placed his hand on it. And I . . . I moved my hand and settled it onto his. He looked into my eyes to see if it was okay, then leaned in and kissed me. Once, softly. I closed my eyes, stopped hearing, shut down all my senses but the nerve endings in my lips. Felt him there. Felt the space after. Felt my own smile as I opened my eyes.

He loosened me then, with a gentle "Can I kiss you again?" My caution eased. The bad tension turned into good tension. He raised his hand so that my ear was in the crook of his palm. The edge of his hand settled close to my pulse. I moved my own palm up, matched him. Our homework crushed beneath us.

We kissed in whispers for minutes, our bodies finding hundreds of ways to hold each other. All the while, the muted news screen unfolded the world to us wordlessly. When we let go, we saw a familiar figure stepping up to a podium, a sea of flags waving in front of him.

"Look, it's Stein," Jimmy said. He pressed a button and the sound came on. We rested into each other and watched.

"There is no such thing as equality for some. Equality must be for all. That is what freedom is. That is what liberty is. No human being is born more or less important than any other. How can we allow ourselves to forget that? What simpler truth is there?"

As the crowd cheered, I looked at Stein's husband, Ron, standing by his side.

"Ron's pretty cute, isn't he?" I said. "I mean, for a forty-five-year-old."

But Jimmy wasn't interested in that (although later he'd tell me that, yes, he thought Ron was adorable, especially when little Jeffrey and Jess were around). Instead, he asked me, "Do you believe he can actually do it?"

I knew Jimmy's own answer was yes. But at that moment, I had to tell him what I really thought.

"I'm not sure," I confessed. "I really don't know." I paused for a moment, feeling I had more to say. "I want to believe it. I want to believe there are enough people in this country who agree with us and want to do the right thing. I want to believe that the reign of fear is over, and people want true equality and fairness. But I guess . . . well, I guess I'm still afraid that people's minds can't open that far, that prejudice is too entrenched."

I was worried that Jimmy was going to correct me, that he was going to say I didn't believe enough. Instead, he kissed me again and said, "Well, we're going to have to try, aren't we?" And I knew he was talking about politics, and I also knew he was talking about us.

I didn't promise him anything, but I promised myself. I was going to try.

Now here I was, over a year later, sitting in Mr. Davis's class, in a changed world that our teacher was in no rush to recognize. I kept looking at Jimmy, but he was concentrating on the front of the room, waiting to see what would be thrown our way.

I expected Mr. Davis to yell. But instead he started quietly.

"This is a day," he began, "that will live in infamy. Our country has been attacked from within."

He stopped for a moment and looked at all of us. He appeared genuinely horrified—sleepless, haunted, angry.

"I've had it up to here with this so-called equality," he continued, saying the last word as if it were a curse. "It was bad enough when we called it *tolerance*. What's next? Are we going to start having serial killers elected President? I bet some of you would like that."

I saw Jimmy's posture draw to attention and immediately knew he was going to say something. Part of me wanted to stop him, to prevent the trouble it would lead to. But the better part of me wanted him to speak up . . . because I knew I wouldn't.

"Haven't we already had serial killers as President?" Jimmy said levelly, not bothering to raise his hand. "Insofar as we've had Presidents responsible for needless deaths in a calculated, premeditated way. That's nothing new. If you want to have this conversation, we can start with Andrew Jackson. But before we get to that, I'm interested—do you think you can liken Stein to a criminal because he's gay, or is it the fact that he's Jewish?"

"Oh, you have all the answers now, don't you?" Mr. Davis didn't leave the front of the room, but he turned to face Jimmy directly. This was one of his favorite responses when he was presented with a statement he didn't agree with—*Oh, you have all the answers now, don't you?* Jimmy had already been asked this when he'd pointed out that the Founding Fathers were far from flawless and that the Constitution and Bill of Rights were best viewed as starter documents, not ends in themselves, or else we'd still have slavery, Black people would still be three-fifths citizens, and women wouldn't be voting at all. Mr. Davis viewed this as taking things out of context, but Jimmy insisted it was actually putting them *into* context.

Right now we didn't have the benefit of hundreds of years' worth of hindsight. History was happening in real time, and the only context Mr. Davis would allow was his own.

"Is the world now yours?" he asked Jimmy. "Am I supposed to step aside? Because that's not going to happen." He paused, and for a second I thought he was done. Then he said, almost offhand, "I've had enough of you. Get out of my class."

Jimmy didn't look like he was about to go anywhere. If anything, he sat more firmly in his seat.

"Get out of your class?" he said. "No."

I started to do what I always do when a moment is too much for me—I started noticing the wrong things. That Mr. Davis's tie was green and blue. That Keisha had put down her pen, and it was about to roll off her desk. No, she caught it. And Mr. Davis's voice rose as he said, "No? What, do you think you're in control here? I believe that I'm the teacher, and this is my classroom. Get out."

Jimmy stayed seated, stayed calm. I knew his expressions so well—even the way he breathed—and I couldn't spot a single hesitation, any shade of doubt. All the hesitations and doubts seemed to have been placed within me, fidgeting in my seat, looking to the clock for help, wanting to explode. I imagined Mr. Davis in fake fatigues, thinking war was a game. Re-enacting it as one. Playing at killing.

Jimmy looked Mr. Davis right in the eye and said, his voice barely conversational, "This might be your classroom, Mr. Davis, but this is as much my school as yours. It is as much my town as yours. And it is damn well as much my country as yours."

"Is it?" Mr. Davis snorted. "What have you done for this country, Mr. Jones? Have you fought for it? Have you even supported it? No, you've just tried to tear it down. I've known kids like you all my life. So idealistic. But you have no clue how the world really works. You think you're going to get a great community through equality and kindness? You are going to have your ass handed to you. By China. By Russia. By any country that doesn't give a shit about your *feelings*.

Weakness is never a strength. You might think you're strong right now, but mark my words, you are not. You are nothing more than a small, ungrateful, spoiled *child,* and you are going to get out of my classroom, even if I have to throw you out myself."

Jimmy stood up, looking pleased. I sat there, stunned. I noticed that it was still sunny outside. It was a nice day outside.

"Thank you, Mr. Davis," Jimmy said, holding up his phone, which I imagined had been recording the whole time. "You've given me everything I need." Then he looked at the rest of us and said, "Let's go."

I don't think people really knew what he meant at first. Then he repeated it, motioning us up, and we understood: He wanted us to abandon Mr. Davis in unison.

"The rest of you will remain seated," Mr. Davis warned, "or you will fail this class."

As if to prove his point, he loaded his grade book onto the class screen.

"Who here wants a zero?" he asked.

"Come on," Jimmy said to us, shifting around to look everyone in the eye. Then he turned to Mr. Davis. "This is such classic reign-of-fear behavior. You're threatened, so you threaten us. Well, not now. Not today."

Mira, Keisha, and a few other kids stood up. I quickly joined them.

But more of the class stayed seated.

"What can he do to you?" Jimmy asked. "We're going

to go right now to the principal and let him know exactly what he just said. You can't just attack students. You can't use your power like that."

Mr. Davis wasn't even looking in Jimmy's direction anymore, treating him like he'd already left. "You will fail this class," he repeated to the rest of us. "Your GPA will be lower. Colleges will want you less. I will not write you a single recommendation."

"You're going to be fired," Jimmy said, his voice even, not gloating.

Mr. Davis nearly smiled. "No, Mr. Jones—you're going to be expelled. If one single person leaves this room with you, I will personally see to it that you're expelled."

I wanted to stop it. I wanted to go back a few minutes and convince Jimmy to cut class. I didn't want any of this to be happening. I was standing, but now it felt awkward. Something had to happen one way or the other.

"Let's go," Jimmy said to us again. "You can't just sit there."

"Will you just leave already?" one of the guys in the back of the room—Satch, a good friend of Jesse Marin's—shouted out. A few kids tittered in response.

"Fine," Jimmy said, picking up his things and heading for the door. I picked up my things, too.

"I wouldn't do that if I were you, Mr. Weiss," Mr. Davis said. He no longer looked horrified. He looked pleased.

Jimmy was out the door. I followed. So did Mira, Keisha, and ten other students.

Eleven kids remained.

"So what now?" Mira asked when we were all in the hall.

"The principal's," Jimmy said. I moved next to him, trying to figure out if he felt as shaken as I did.

When I put my hand on his shoulder, he stiffened.

"Are you okay?" I asked quietly.

"You just sat there," he murmured, anger and disappointment in his voice. "You just sat there and didn't say a thing."

Then he walked forward, leaving my hand—me—behind.

"What are we doing?" a girl named Gretchen asked.

"The right thing," I answered, a beat too late.

four

"The personal is political," Jimmy said to me one of the first nights I sneaked over to his house, "and the political is personal. We vote every time we make a choice. We vote with our lives."

I pulled closer to him under the blanket, ran my hand down his bare chest. Voting.

"Mr. Davis should not have said those things," Principal Cotter said to us now, after listening to the recording. "But you shouldn't have walked out of class, either."

"Bastard," Jimmy said when we left Principal Cotter's office, with an assurance that Mr. Davis would be called to

account for his actions, and that we wouldn't be failed or expelled.

"I'm sorry," I said when the next bell rang and everyone else had gone to their next classes.

"Today is a part of what America was meant to be," President-Elect Stein said on the news sites. *"Justice. Equality. Democracy. We know what we have to do . . . and we will do it."*

"I know you are," Jimmy said. "I know."

"This is just the beginning," Stein told us. And I realized that, yes, he was right. I had started the day thinking it was the ending. But really it was the beginning.

"I can't believe it," Jimmy told me during second period. We'd both dodged out of study hall and were sitting in a corner of the library, our own temporary refuge. "I can't believe Principal Cotter didn't understand."

"Maybe that's what history is," I said, thinking about everything that had happened in the last twenty-four hours.

"You go from one *I can't believe it* to the next. And some-times the *I can't believe it*s are good, and sometimes they're bad. But when the sum total of positive ones outweighs the negative ones, that's progress. You can't let this one *I can't believe it* get you down—Stein's still going to be President. Mr. Davis can't change that, as much as he wants to."

It felt good to be surrounded by books, by all this solid knowledge, by these objects that could be ripped page by page but couldn't be torn if the pages all held together. So much of the information we received was ephemeral— pixels on screen, words passing in the air. But here I felt that thoughts had weight.

We scrolled some more on our phones—the full spec-trum of reactions, from celebration in some parts of the country to outbursts of hate in others. None of it was sur-prising, nor was it surprising that not everyone seemed to be going along with the election. The faith in the process had been undermined by years of propaganda. There were still plenty of people who felt the truth could be refused if you didn't agree with it.

Kansas was the only place where the vote had been close enough for this disputation of facts to matter. The governor—a member of the opposition party—was de-manding a recount even though Stein's victory was over the legal threshold . . . and it looked like he would get his way.

"How're you guys doing back there?" a voice asked. We looked up and saw Ms. Kaye, our school librarian. She'd had a Stein/Martinez bumper sticker on her car since early

January, so we knew where she stood. I'm sure we would've figured it out easily enough even without the bumper sticker; Ms. Kaye was that wonderful kind of librarian who loved her kids even more than she loved her books. She knew why she was here, and we knew it, too. We couldn't help but want to grow up to be just like her.

"We're okay," Jimmy told her.

"Okay? You're not usually one to answer with typical teenage understatement, James. What's going on?"

He told her what had happened in Mr. Davis's class.

"That *bastard*," Ms. Kaye said. "Not that you just heard that from me. But don't worry—there are plenty of us here who aren't going to let that slide. Cotter's stupid, but he's not that stupid. Anyway, don't let it ruin today. We should all be celebrating. You know how old I am? Sixty-five. And the world continues to amaze me, no more so than on a day like today. I'm not talking down to you when I say you can't begin to understand what this means. When I was born, women were told to stay at home. White people were a much bigger majority in this country. Very few people questioned their sexuality or their gender, because no one had given them the vocabulary or the encouragement to do so. A woman like Alice Martinez being Vice President? Forget it. And Abe Stein as President? When pigs fly! But I'm telling you—pigs now fly. I can press thirteen buttons on a phone every morning and see my sister in Borneo. I can find out what they're talking about in a small town in France. You can buy raspberries in any country in the world, on any day. You can get a vaccine to help you against the flu, and you can walk down the street without being made to fear that the sky will fall. Pigs flying—that's nothing compared to this. You don't realize—the great thing about change is how quickly we get used to it. So I'm not complaining. The more things change, the more they don't stay the same. Don't let anyone tell you otherwise. They might not change everywhere all at once—but there are moments when the impossible becomes the inevitable, and the rest is just a matter of time."

I was grateful to hear her say this. But I still didn't think I was off the hook for not speaking up earlier. Even if Jimmy had said it was okay, it didn't feel okay. I wanted to tell him this. I waited until Ms. Kaye gave us another big congratulations on the day, then eased off to another kid in another corner.

I knew I had to say something more than sorry. Not for Jimmy, really—more for myself.

"Back there," I began, "in class. I didn't know what to do. I froze. It was like I couldn't do anything but watch. Even though it was killing me."

Jimmy looked at me for a second, then said, "You don't blink, you know that?"

I blinked. "What do you mean?"

He smiled. "When you're being sincere. It's like you're so busy getting the words out that you forget to blink. It's sweet."

Now, of course, I was ultraconscious of every blink.

"So it's not" (blink) "what I" (blink) "say, it's" (blink) "how many times" (blink) "—oh, damn" (stare) (blink).

"Now you're even cuter. Just because I become all confrontational doesn't mean you have to be that way. Not until it really matters, okay?"

I'd been so insecure when we first started going out. I'd spent so much time counting. How many times he kissed me first versus how many times I kissed him first. How late I'd stay up for a text from him versus how late he'd stay up for word from me. How many friends of his liked me versus how many of my friends liked him. No matter what the tally was, I always lost. I was always thinking in terms of *too much* or *not enough,* rarely allowing myself that crucial space in between. Except when he was around. Except when we were really together. Then I could forget—I couldn't turn it off, but I could forget to turn it on. Gradually, the columns began to tip. I lost track of keeping track. In order to let us be, I let myself be.

But there were still some moments, moments like this one, when I felt the despair of that *not enough,* of the forgiveness I wouldn't allow myself to take.

Jimmy knew this, and, just like me, he didn't know what to do about it. He could only tell me it was all right. I was the one who had to feel it.

I leaned my head onto his shoulder. He leaned his head on top of mine. We checked the news until the period ended and it was time to go back to class.

*

"... *When asked to define his vision of the Great Community, Stein said it was based on the simple premise of 'love thy neighbor.'*

"*'We are not taught "love thy neighbor unless their skin is a different color from yours" or "love thy neighbor unless they don't make as much money as you do" or "love thy neighbor unless they don't share your beliefs." We are taught "love thy neighbor." No exceptions. We are all in this together—every single one of us. And the only way we are going to survive as a society is through compassion. A Great Community does not mean we all think the same things or do the same things. It simply means we are willing to work together and are willing to love despite our differences.'*

"*Stein says he has no doubt that this can happen.*

"*'People do this every day of their lives on a small scale. I'm just asking them to do it on a bigger scale. When a disaster happens—when an earthquake hits, or our country is under attack—we rally ourselves to be a Great Community. Well, there's no reason we have to wait for bad in order to recognize good. The Great Community will happen, and it will happen in our lifetime. . . .'*"

five

Happily, the Jesus Freaks saved seats for us at lunch.

Jesus Freak was their term, not mine—Janna said it was in honor of the song "I Freak Out for Jesus" by the band Holy Ghostwriter, one of the bigger Jesus Revolution pop acts. I took her word for it—there wasn't really a Jewish equivalent of Holy Ghostwriter, and if there had been, I can't say that I would've listened to it. I was more of a grunk fan myself.

Janna and Mandy said a prayer over their cafeteria food, thanking Jesus for the bounty of synthetic meat and cola-free cola on their trays. I surprised them (and Jimmy) by joining in their "Amen" at the end. I figured I owed Jesus a little thanks, because it was doubtful we'd have a gay Jewish president if it weren't for him and his followers.

What Would Jesus Do? It all started with that simple question. The way I understand it, the phrase had been around for a while. People used to wear it on T-shirts, or wore the letters *WWJD* on bracelets, with the telltale question mark on a bead at the end. It started on a personal level—girls would ask themselves *WWJD?* if their boyfriends wanted to have sex with them, or husbands would ask *WWJD?* if they wanted to calm down before yelling at their wives.

But then other things happened. Pandemics and hurricanes. Shootings and wildfires. Kids killed in elementary schools. Whole cities nearly submerged by oceans and seas. Millions of people dead. The Decents and their program of Denial Education reached their peak, especially in the channels of social media and news that they controlled. But every person who died, every person who suffered, left a crack in the wall they were trying to build. Suddenly people started to ask it again—*What Would Jesus Do?* And this time it wasn't just on a personal level—it was on a political level, too.

For the Jesus Revolutionaries, the answer was clear: Jesus would not be withholding medicine from people who could not afford it. Jesus would not call the importance of medical treatment into question. He would not cast stones at people of races, sexual orientations, or genders other than his own. He would not demonize people just because they came from another country. He would not condone the failing, viperous, scandal-plagued hierarchy of some churches and most governments. Jesus would welcome everyone to his table. He would love them, and he would find peace.

People wanted to hear this. People needed to hear this. And they needed to feel it, too.

Janna's parents had been involved from the start—taking part, as Janna liked to say, as their church reformed "under the new management of Jesus." Mandy's family had been nonbelievers until they found themselves a part of the movement; Mandy's father was out of work, their mother was undergoing treatment for cancer, and Mandy was, as they'd later tell me, losing their place in life. It was a time when it was easy to believe the worst in the world. The reign of fear had done that to us. We thought any bridge could break, any stranger could do us harm. But then the Jesus Revolutionaries started to make themselves heard. They'd always been around, but they'd been overshadowed by the vast hierarchy that had tried to keep them in their place. For Mandy's family, the revelation came when Mandy's aunt had taken them to her church. There, in the congregation, things fell into place. This was a new gospel to them—one that glorified empathy over condemnation, one that sang exaltation rather than exhortation, one where Mandy was invited in rather than shut out for refusing to be binary. Suddenly the concept of love shone like a beacon . . . and Mandy followed it until it led them here, on this day.

Janna and Mandy had a third friend, Cathy, who did not share their faith. Lately she'd become a Decent, wanting to go back to the old church and the old ways. She changed her name to Mary Catherine and started coming to school in shapeless black dresses, looking like a songless nun and acting like one, too. At first, Janna and Mandy had tried to stay friends with her, but Mary Catherine seemed determined to thwart their attempts. She wouldn't talk to them—not when they called, not when they wrote, not when they came up to her and said hi. It was as if her only way to deny change was to deny friendship and happiness.

I looked over now to the corner of the cafeteria where she usually sat, twisting a wire tightly around her finger. She didn't talk to anyone anymore, still falling under the Decent belief that self-negation equaled wisdom, that silence equaled knowledge, that disengagement somehow meant love. Her fingers had ridges from all the times she'd wrapped the wire around them.

I turned back to Janna and saw that she, too, was watching Mary Catherine. She often did, and it always made her sad.

"I still want to say something to her," she told me now. "Isn't that stupid?"

"It's not stupid," I said. Mandy, Jimmy, and the others were preoccupied with talking about the election, so Janna and I could have our own conversation in the crowd.

"Even today. We're all talking about community. And there she is, at the other end of the room, and we might as well speak different languages. Last year she would have been right here with us. She would have been happy, Duncan. I know it."

"Look, Janna—you tried," I reminded her.

"I know. I tried, and I prayed, and I tried some more and prayed some more. But then I realized: In order for us to be so far apart, she must have been praying in the opposite direction. How do you do that, Duncan? Pray to have someone out of your life. Pray for a friendship to be over. There are times—oh, never mind."

"What?"

"It's dumb."

"C'mon," I said.

Janna scrunched up her nose. "Fine. There are times I think of us all and I wish we were back in second grade. Not really that young. But I wish it felt like second grade. I'm not saying everyone was friends back then. But we all got along. There were groups, but they didn't really divide. At the end of the day, your class was your class, and you felt like you were a part of it. You had your friends and you had the other kids, but you didn't really hate anyone longer than a couple of hours. Everybody got a birthday card. In second grade, we were all in it together. Now we're all apart. We're no better than the grown-ups."

She kept watching Mary Catherine as she said this. Mary Catherine, I was sure, didn't even look up.

I remembered being friends with Jesse Marin in second grade, going over to his house and acting like superheroes, playing games for hours that seemed endless until the abrupt time came for me to go home. I was sure I got into fights in second grade, but I couldn't remember a single one. Unlike now, when all I could see were the conflicts I had with people. When I looked at Mary Catherine, I saw her wall of silence. When I passed Jesse in the hall, I felt all the bad things he thought about me and all the bad things I thought back about him.

But then I would be with Janna, and it seemed better. Because, really, Janna and I never felt like we were meant to be friends. I wasn't really a part of her crowd, and I didn't really have my own crowd for her to be a part of. She still dotted her *i*'s with full circles and felt genuinely thankful for every sunny day. I believed more in dark clouds, in sharp dots, in needing proof in order to feel trust. The fact that I was gay and Jewish wasn't a problem for her—she was a true embracer, and wouldn't have thought to qualify that with any categories. But there were moments when I had to admit that I wasn't sure I could embrace as widely. My grudges could be too fierce for that. Even if I never did anything but hold them inside.

I was Jewish, but I wasn't sure about God. I believed in the long line—the lineage—of being Jewish. I believed in lighting candles on Shabbat when I was home, in celebrating Rosh Hashanah with apples and honey for a sweet new year, in fasting on Yom Kippur and reflecting on the things I'd done and the things I needed to do better. I believed in our history as outsiders, and the strength it took to overcome attack after attack after attack. But did this history lead me to faith? I wasn't sure.

The reign of fear was raging as I was growing up. There must have been some ashes I'd breathed in, some remnants that would not be washed down.

I saw Jesse and Satch and their gang sniggering at their table. They kept saying the word *Kansas,* and I could tell from their expressions that they felt the election wasn't over yet. Jesse made some Stein jokes and made sure everyone in the cafeteria could hear them—"What do you call it when Stein's husband has sex with him? Fill-a-Stein. Get it?"—and I had to say to myself, *They're only trying to make us afraid again. If we're not intimidated by them, they have no power.*

"It's why *loser* has stayed an insult for so long," I said to Janna, who along with the rest of the table was very aware of what Jesse and his group were doing. "Calling someone a loser is a way of saying you've won without having to actually win anything."

"Don't listen to them," Jimmy told me. "This time they've lost."

But I would've believed it more if they looked like they'd lost. Or acted like they'd lost.

"Do they know something we don't?" I asked.

"No," Janna said emphatically.

Luckily, the conversation was turned by the arrival of Gus, who had to be my favorite Mexican American gay Jesus Freak postconsumer activist. None of his clothes had labels, but he always made sure they fit really, really well. You could see almost every chest and stomach muscle underneath his plum-pink shirt, as well as the small Jesus that always hung from his neck.

"Who made y'all such doomster gloomsters? We must cel-e-brate!"

"We're just worried about Kansas," Mandy admitted.

"Kansas *Kansas*," Gus said dismissively. "That governor won't do nada. If he tries, he'll have a higher power to answer to—and I'm not talking 'bout Stein. C'mon—how 'bout we swing by the ghost mall before we go to the victory party? That's how we know for sure that the election is secure: The party's still on."

Gus had been a volunteer at campaign headquarters with us. He'd started off on the phone banks . . . until it became obvious that he was confusing some of the older voters with the rapid enthusiasm with which he talked. So instead he became a Stein street preacher, chatting up people face to face, winning some over with the facts and a smile.

I also started off on the phone banks, and also switched away from them—but for a totally different reason. I thought I'd be fine at first—all we really had to do was talk to random citizens and upload them Stein's position papers if they had specific questions, like "How will Stein compensate for the fuel crisis in Dry Alaska?" or "Where does Stein stand on Jesus in schools?" or even "Why should I vote for a gay guy?" I figured I could handle it.

But then I started making the calls, and I was shocked by how mean the people could be. We were careful not to call during dinnertime or too late, so they weren't angry because of that. No—they heard what I was saying and immediately started lashing out. Not everyone, certainly. There were plenty of people who didn't support Stein but still supported common courtesy. Even though I disagreed with those people, I appreciated them. It was the others—the people who felt it was their right to attack—who volted me. It was worse if they had the cameras on, so I had to get yelled at face to face. One of the conservative influencers (din-fluencers?) had told his listeners to stick their double asshalfs at us if we called. That wasn't too bad—we took screenshots and printed out our favorite rude butt shots. It was just stupid. But the anger, the yelling, the names I was called just for being a Stein supporter by people I'd never met—that wasn't stupidity as much as loathing and fear.

This was my weakness: I couldn't stand meanness. It unnerved me.

With people like Jesse, it was one thing; I knew them, and expected it, and knew that even if they wanted to make me look like a fool, they didn't actually wish me harm. But some of the people I called—I felt they would've killed me if they could have. Maybe not in the sense that they'd hold a gun to my face and pull the trigger. But if they had a button they could press to make me disappear, without having to see the mess, they'd press it. Not because of my specific self, but because of the things I believed in and some of the things I was. One guy with a big Decent cross hanging on the wall behind him told me he wished that AIDS was still untreatable, so me and Stein and "the rest of you" could come down with it. One woman told me I was the downfall of America, and that if Stein was elected it was only a short time until we were invaded by Europe and Asia—"unless, of course, he gets all the other Jews to help him." Another woman asked me if I was having sex with Stein, if I was his "little butt boy." She said this as she held a baby in her arms.

And I was speechless. I literally didn't know what to say. I knew that hanging up on them would only give them the satisfaction that they'd won our encounter—since that's what they'd made it, a conflict to win or lose. So I wouldn't hang up. I would just sit there, silent, as they told me I was against God, against America, against Family, against Decency. Eventually they'd tire themselves out or realize I wasn't going to say anything back, and they'd hang up. But even when they did, it didn't feel like I'd won. Only one time—this one woman started attacking me for being immoral and disgusting. I shut myself down and just watched. Then, in midsentence, she stopped. She stared at my face in the screen, actually took the time to look at me and how old I was, and she stopped. Our eyes met over our screens and she couldn't go on. She didn't say sorry; she didn't apologize for taking things out on me. But she stopped. And stepped back. And hung up.

That made me feel a little better, but only until the next mean response. I found myself only calling the people who were coded as Stein/Martinez supporters. They thanked me, but most of them didn't understand why I was calling since we already had their votes. Finally I gave up. I'd wander over to Jimmy's phone booth and stand in a corner where the phonecam wouldn't spot me.

Of course, Jimmy was better at this than I was. He was charming with the Stein supporters and more charming with the all-important Undecideds, especially the ones who wanted to talk. When he was mooned, he would say a polite "Thank you very much for your contribution" before hanging up, and save his laughter for later. With the mean people, I could definitely see a tension—but he could control it. Again, he'd manage to stay polite—"With all due respect, you're wrong about that" and "That's simply not correct" and "If you would read the Stein position paper on that issue, you'd see that what you've heard is erroneous." Even when they got graphic in their insults, he refused to let them see him riled. He would say "I don't think there's any call for that kind of language" before hanging up, so that their offensiveness became the cause to end the call. Only after the call had been disconnected would he unleash a string of his own graphic insults, until he was calm enough to make the next call.

This, I guessed, was politics.

He didn't say anything about me being in the back of the booth, so I hovered there until Gus popped in and said he was going to hit the streets. I knew Jimmy would be cool about me staying with him, but I also knew that every call he made would mean a call I wasn't making. I didn't want to feel that defeated, and I didn't know how to tell him about it, because clearly it was something that wasn't bothering him as much. So I decided to act like I'd planned all along to join Gus in his canvassing. I'd still be dealing with strangers, but this time I'd have someone by my side. Someone talkative.

We had an easy assignment—to head to Gus's church to make sure everyone was registered to vote. We got there right before people arrived for mass.

"Let's go inside and say hi to Pastor Graciela," Gus said.

I'd never been inside Gus's church before. It had been built in one of the buildings that used to house those old-fashioned power generators. All the heavy equipment had been moved out, and the result was an abundance of space. Everything—the section of comfortable chairs in the middle, the long colorful chains that dangled the lights from the ceiling—seemed designed to make you feel like you were part of something larger, without being made to feel small.

Over the altar, where a crucifix would preside in most churches, there was a beautiful statue of Jesus, peacefully watching over everyone who wandered in, his face showing sympathy, patience, wisdom. Even though it was carved in stone, his eyes shone bright. I was Jewish, but I was still familiar enough with all the old paintings and the old ways to be struck by this.

"You're seeing?" Gus said. "You expect there to be a cross there. But what matters to us, and what mattered to God, is Jesus's life, not his death. A miracle happened, but the miracle happened because of who Jesus was. The point is to live like him, not to die like him."

He reached to the thin chain around his neck and pulled the small gold Jesus out from under his shirt. I saw that Jesus was in a pose similar to the one above the altar. "Take a look. That's love. Compassion. That's why we care about him. That's why he was special."

As he put the necklace back where it had been, as close to his body as anything could be, a woman wearing a purple robe walked over to us. She was no taller than my shoulder and her hair was dotted with gray. I figured she was the pastor. I knew that churches like Gus's used to call their priests Father, until the Jesus Revolution and the decision that titles like Father and Mother needed to be retired. ("Pastor Michael isn't my father," Janna once said to me. "Why would I call him that? There are other ways of showing respect without creating these weird family power roles.")

Pastor Graciela welcomed me, then gently told Gus that although she of course supported what he was doing, there couldn't be any campaigning inside the church. Whatever we wanted to say, it had to be outside.

"Absolutely," Gus told her. "We just wanted to say hey."

After a few minutes of talking with Pastor Graciela, we headed outside. People were just starting to arrive for mass—not too many of them, but enough to spark some conversations. Gus was at the center of our invisible stage on the steps, with me half curtained beside him. Mostly I watched. I watched as we got kind nods and small words of affirmation. I watched as other congregants took Gus by the arm and swore to him that they'd be there on election day. This was the kind of swearing I could stand, not the kind I'd been attacked with on the phone. I started to get back some of my faith in people. Here, and later in the week when Gus and I stood outside my synagogue and did pretty much the same thing, and at least a dozen other times when I worked with Stein supporters or met people who respectfully disagreed, I felt the work that the mean people had done on my mind becoming undone. Because that's the thing about mean people: They make you think that the world will never work, that there are divides you will fall into if you approach. It takes a whole lot of good people to fill in the breach created by a single mean one.

"It's our future!" Gus would sing to anyone who came past. "You've got to participate in our future!" His belief in this was so strong that it made his body dance. He would sway in his no-logo jeans and whirl from person to person with the Jesus figure shifting along with his heart. I wondered if this, really, was how he stayed so fit.

Even when the election was over, his buzz of energy remained.

"C'mon, my friends," he said to us now. "I'll meet you by the doors as soon as the school releases us."

Mira and Keisha said they'd have to meet us at Stein headquarters for the victory party, since they had basketball practice after school. But Mandy, Jimmy, Janna, and I said we were in for a quick run to the ghost mall. The point of places like the ghost mall was for us to be together . . . and being together was exactly the point we wanted to make right now.

six

On the way over, we loaded one of Stein's old speeches and listened.

"If we can be caring individuals, why can't we be a caring society? If we can build our lives on the foundation of kindness and love, why can't we build our country on the same foundations? Is this idealistic? By all means, yes! We as a country have always had ideals, and we should live by our ideals. Life. Liberty. The pursuit of happiness. What are these if not expressions of kindness and love, of caring and compassion? There is nothing wrong with idealism. You can't tell me that we as people are motivated by greed or hatred or jealousy. You cannot tell me that we do not care for one another. Parents care for children. Children care for parents. Brother cares for sister, sister for brother. Not always, but most of the time. What satisfaction

does a dentist get from being a dentist? He is paid well, yes. But the satisfaction comes from knowing he makes his patients' lives easier. What satisfaction does a builder get from being a builder? She makes a structure that will last, yes. But she gets her satisfaction knowing that it will give people shelter, that it will be of some worth to their lives. We all want to make the world a better place. We all want to matter, and we know that what matters is caring. What matters is the difference you make in the lives of the people around you and generations to come. We know this on an individual scale. We must also know this as a nation, and as citizens of the world."

One of the key ingredients of the reign of fear has been disembodiment.

The theory behind this is simple. It is much harder to attack someone in person. It is much harder to lie to someone in person. It is much harder to deny the humanity of someone who is standing right in front of you, undeniably human. (I'm not saying it's impossible. It is very possible. It's just harder.)

Our bodies are designed for human interaction. When we don't get it, we become lonely. When we become lonely, fear speaks to us in a louder voice. The politicians and the corporations behind the reign knew this. Separated from other people, we will buy more, to quell that loneliness. Separated from other people, we will argue more, to feel the power of our own assertions. We will crave more attention.

We will want to have followers, gather likes, because we will use those things to (momentarily) make us feel less lonely. We will broadcast ourselves because otherwise all we feel is void. When nothing is in person, we are vulnerable to all kinds of manipulation. We think we are building our own virtual space, but the manipulators are providing all the furniture, all the walls.

Even though it's been a few years, I remember what it was like in lockdown, what it was like to not see my friends. Now I think, *Look at what happened when no one could see their friends.* People who weren't their friends entrenched them on sides of various arguments, because arguing gave them a rush. Social media set up a toxic popularity contest, and you had to compete in it alone.

When the insurrection attempts came, I could almost understand it. Those people storming the Capitol, banding together to threaten democracy—they were euphoric because finally they could hang out in a crowd of their friends again.

We'd been told this story: Each generation would love technology more and more, would depend on technology more and more, would be happier and happier in a virtual space. And for sure, there were plenty of kids my age who lost themselves in worlds of "content"—a noun masquerading as an adjective. Our phones functioned as a body part. But ultimately, this idea that we'd fall so willingly into technology's embrace was a "truth" designed by technology companies, not by us. The lockdowns were a wake-up call.

This is what it would feel like if we didn't have each other anymore, if we stopped being bodies and relied entirely on being whatever we projected onto other people's screens.

My friends and I didn't want to disempower ourselves into data. We wanted to be in person as much as we could.

That's why we went to the ghost mall. It was never busy, and it was always a little sad. There wasn't anything inside that we couldn't buy online. But buying online didn't involve any senses besides sight. And buying online couldn't be shared in the same way.

If there was one thing making me a little nervous as we headed to the ghost mall, it was the fact that Jimmy's birthday was coming up in a few days, and I still hadn't gotten him anything. I knew I could (and would) donate to one of his registered charities, but I also wanted to give him something he could hold in his hand. It didn't have to be expensive, only valued.

We were jammed against each other in the backseat of Gus's Prius, Jimmy half sitting on my lap and me half stroking his wrist, playing with his bracelet. We had been going out long enough for our affections to be casual. I no longer looked for meaning in every touch, every gesture. Only the unusual ones.

When Stein's old speech was done, Janna called out, "Gus, can you load up 'Lord Enuff 4 Me'? Please please please!"

Jimmy leaned back into me a little harder and I tried not to roll my eyes or laugh. We were so stuck. Perhaps the biggest test a friendship can face is when one of the friends wants to blast a truly crap song.

As Janna, Gus, and Mandy yell-sang the chorus ("Baby, you don't need 2 B / Lording it over me, / 'cause any fool can C / the Lord is Lord Enuff 4 Me"), Jimmy leaned over to me and whispered, "Do you think we can get Stein to ban this music?"

I said we could only hope.

Luckily, we arrived at the mall before the next Holy Ghostwriter song ("Baby B My Sunbeam") started to play.

I thought for one evil second of getting *Holy Ghostwriter's Most Inspired Hits* for Jimmy for his birthday. But that would have been too cruel—he would have felt bad deleting it, so it would've haunted him every time he went to shuffle.

No—I needed something he would love. I was a little uncomfortable when nothing immediately sprang to mind. For a second I found myself envying Keisha and Mira. Not only could they finish each other's sentences—they could finish each other's paragraphs. Even though they lived in two different houses, it was like they had only one wardrobe, mixing and matching so often we had no memory of which clothes were Mira's and which were Keisha's. In April, Keisha had arranged for Mira's favorite author to give them a call for their birthday; the hour-long conversation was the present. And in June, Mira had given Keisha a sweater they'd spent almost a whole year making, having taught themself to knit in order to do it. For my birthday in May, Jimmy had planted me a tree, right outside my bedroom window. (My parents were a little surprised, but they let me keep it.) I wanted to do something just as cool, but the only ideas I had were everybody else's ideas.

I hoped to find some direction in the mall. As we'd expected, we were practically the only people inside who didn't work there. During the holiday season it was more crowded, and maybe that's how they stayed in business. But on an average November afternoon like today, it felt like walking through the ruins of an ancient civilization, a museum dedicated to the short era when humans had to walk into a store in order to buy something.

The first shop we stopped in was a fragrance store, which wasn't a whole lot of help in my search. They had a scent bar where you could create your own, but I didn't want Jimmy to smell like anything other than his usual mix of shampoo and body heat and spark.

The scent of the season was marshmallow, and Janna spent a good amount of time experimenting with the different kinds before deciding that lightly browned was her favorite.

Next we went to the jeans store. Gus couldn't get there fast enough. Just as I predicted, he went directly to the newest style of you-fit jeans. He loved the way the denim contracted to mold against his body, then expanded to let him back out again.

I was lucky Jimmy hadn't really known me in seventh grade, during my Period of Indecisive Style (as Mandy liked to call it). It had happened after Jesse Marin and a lot of the other guys started to outgrow their friendships with me, and I hadn't yet figured out which new friendships I was going to grow into. Having read a few too many of Mandy's advice blogs, I decided the problem was that I really didn't have my own style. So I experimented. First came the Sports Irony look, where I mimicked Jesse's baseball wear but upped it two notches too much. That struck out. Then I decided I would only wear that season's big fashion push . . . which, unfortunately, was the W-neck T-shirt, heralding the Jagged Collar phase. As winter approached, I decided to layer— with a white shirt always on top and stripes or patterns always underneath. The Hidden Meaning look, which then turned into Mix-and-Not-Match when I ran out of white shirts. I spent a week in flannel hoodies—Badass Lumber-jack. Then I started wearing things inside out. That lasted two weeks, mostly because bullies kept pulling on the tags. Spring came, and I thought it would be cool to wear shirts that mimicked street signs. My Yield Caution phase.

The end came quickly. I ordered a One Way T-shirt, and once it arrived I realized the arrow pointed to my crotch. When Mandy came over later that day, I held it up and asked them what I was doing. They told me I'd always had a style; I just needed to realize that style was like personality—it didn't always have to be consistent; it just had to be something you lived with. I asked them how they knew that. They said they'd read it on an advice blog. Then they helped me bring all the W-necks to Goodwill.

Now I didn't try to have a style. There were just things I liked and things I didn't like. It made shopping much easier.

I watched as Jimmy wandered off to the retro section, holding up a pair of pleated stonewashed jeans and taunting me to try them on. Again, I thought about how I could be evil and come back and purchase them for his birthday. I knew Jimmy was really eyeing a pair of never-wash jeans, but I wasn't sure never-wash said *I love you* the way I wanted to.

"Check me out!" Gus called. He'd come out of the changing booth wearing a pair of you-fit 5143s.

Mandy turned bright red. Janna giggled.

"You might want to set them a little looser," Jimmy suggested. "And wear underwear."

"I *am* wearing underwear!" Gus said. "But it's no-line!" As we shook our heads, he headed back into the booth, emerging next with a pair of cordlessuroy pants and a fuchsia top, followed by a retro concert shirt for a band called TV Dinner.

Since Gus had actual-purchased a pair of no-label you-fit 5142s when they'd come out last month, it was easier than it normally would have been for him to let the sales guy take the 5143s away from him and instead donate them to a kid in a homeless center who had them on a wish list.

"Hombre, that was a big donation," he said as we walked out. "I can't believe how much those jeans cost. But, hey, it's Stein Day. I don't mind giving a little more."

While Jimmy and the others headed to the bookstore,

I sneaked next door to the lamp emporium. Jimmy didn't exactly need a lamp—it's not like he was living in total darkness or anything. But I was getting desperate. I went immediately to the back corner that held all the misfit lamps. Lava gurgled. Neon flamingos perched. They even had a few in the shape of legs.

I sighed.

This was too hard.

The evil presents were looking better and better.

When I got to the bookstore, I could immediately tell that something was wrong. Jimmy was watching something on his phone, and he looked like he'd just been told a pet had died.

"What is it?" I said, rushing over.

"It's Kansas," he replied. The way he said it, I just wanted to hold him tight. But I also knew from the way he said it that he wasn't ready to be held. There was too much anger and disappointment and confusion to get out first before he could let himself give way a little.

Our friends were around us now, pulling out their phones and loading up the news.

"In a startlingly swift move, Governor Nicols of Kansas an-
nounced that he had confiscated all the voting machines in the
state and would begin his own recount. He said he had reason

to believe the reported results were false, and that he had 'grave doubts' that Stein would end up victorious. Such a reversal would change the outcome of yesterday's election."

"How can he do that?" Mandy asked, her voice barely a whisper.

Soon it became clear: The head of the Kansas Election Commission was one of the governor's cronies, and both said they had "discovered" enough problems with voting sites and absentee ballots to declare a recount. Their goal: to disqualify enough Stein voters to swing the election.

"You can bet they're altering votes as we speak," Jimmy said disgustedly. "Stein won fair and square, and they know it."

Hearing Stein's voice, we tuned back in.

"I want to assure all Americans that I will, in no uncertain terms, fight this partisan attack on a fair election. Every indication we have shows that our party won Kansas decisively and without any controversy. The truth must be heeded. The American people will not be deceived by wishful thinking and willful manipulation. We will not take this lying down."

We wandered around the ghost mall for a little while longer, checking our phones frequently for updates.

"Should we head to the party?" I asked.

There was a silence until Janna finally said what we were all thinking:

"Are you sure there's still going to be a party?"

"Hello, yes!" Gus said, sounding shocked. "Last time I checked, Stein was elected to be the next President of the United S. of A. We're gonna be popping some corks."

"That's the spirit!" Mandy chimed.

"Hallelujah!" Janna echoed, sounding a little less convinced but still hoping strong.

Only Jimmy seemed fully doubtful, and I teetered in between him and the rest of them.

"What do you think?" I asked.

"I think we should go to the party," he replied, smiling slightly. "It's not the end of the world until it's the end of the world."

seven

We piled back into Gus's car and drove over to Stein's local headquarters. We'd done this so many times before— "going on a mission," Jimmy liked to call it. Sometimes there'd be as many as eight people in Gus's four-seater, making our way to volunteer in any way possible. From the moment we'd read on Stein's site that a headquarters was being made for our area, we wanted to be a part of it. I was a little worried that they'd scoff at us, since we couldn't even vote yet. I expected them to have us bring them coffee, clean out the trash, hang posters around town—things like that. But from the minute we arrived, we were made to feel like our contributions mattered, and that we were just as able to spread the word as people five times our age.

Part of this was because of the mood Stein and Martinez brought to the campaign. And part of it was because of Virgil and Sara, who'd practically lived at the headquarters over the past few months and ran it as if it was their one big shot at changing the world for the better. Virgil was about my grandfather's age, but there were moments when he'd leap down the stairs or slap you a five that felt like fifteen, and you'd wonder if he was really a twenty-year-old in a wizened disguise. Sara *was* a twenty-year-old, a drop-dead-then-come-back-to-life-gorgeous lesbian who'd taken a semester off from college to work full-time for the campaign. I'd had a nonsexual crush on her almost immediately; on the first day we came to the campaign, she wasn't flustered when I got flustered about the prospect of talking to strangers. Instead of showing me to the door, she showed me to the kitchen, feeding me cookies from an honest-to-goodness cookie jar and explaining to me that our job wasn't to argue voters into supporting Stein, it was to provide them with the information they needed to make the right choice. I figured I'd be okay providing information, and I also figured I'd be okay sitting in the kitchen with this generous college student, talking about books and music and the fourteen steps to alleviating the deficit that rich-people tax cuts had caused.

The Stein/Martinez headquarters was located in a house on a suburban street in the town next to mine, just off Route 280. The couple who'd lived in it had moved to Florida, and instead of putting it on the market right away, they'd lent it to the campaign. As a result, going to work there was almost like heading over to a friend's house to visit; after a few times, you started to get a sense of where things were, but there were still moments when it was confusing.

We all used the side door to get in. This time, unpiling from Gus's car, we could hear music blasting inside. Virgil's wife, Flora, was the first person we saw, standing in the kitchen surrounded by bowls of guilt-free and guilt-plus snacks.

"Hello there!" she said, then gave each of us big hugs. "Everyone's in the living room. We've cleared the desks out so there can be some dancing and thrumping."

Gus was an ace thrumper, but I wasn't sure this was the time or the place. Was it possible to thrump when Kansas was in play?

Flora's spirits seemed high enough. But when we got to the living room, it was clear that the people inside weren't as certain of victory as the decorations were. A banner read CONGRATULATIONS! on top of the big screen, but the muted newsreaders were miming a different story.

"Hey, guys," Mira called. Instinctively, I looked next to them for Keisha, but she wasn't there.

"Where's your other half?" I asked.

"Around. Helping out as usual," Mira answered. "That girl never rests."

We tried to chat with some of the other volunteers, but the scroll on the screen kept distracting us. While most of us tried to go through the motions of a party, Virgil stood in the middle of the room, watching the news and saying, "This isn't going to happen again. There's no way we're going to let this happen again."

I knew Virgil had been part of the movement to abolish

the electoral college. The movement's continual defeat was, as Stein liked to point out in his speeches, a watershed moment of self-interest triumphing over the national interest. In order for the amendment to pass, it needed to be ratified by the populations of at least a few of the smaller states that would have lost their unfair advantage. (Since every state has two senators, these small states automatically get two more votes in the electoral college than they should have received for a population their size, making it unfair.) Not a single small state had pledged to shift to the popular vote, no matter how many appeals were made. And there was no way to get around that, so the electoral college stayed, sticking us with more elections where the person who received the most votes didn't necessarily win the Presidency. This was not democracy, but each time it happened, people just went along with it. Except people like Virgil. He was constantly telling us that there was a long tradition in America of righting the wrongs of the Founding Fathers, making people more equal when it came to voting. After the Fifteenth Amendment and the Nineteenth Amendment, the amendment for direct elections was the last hurdle for electoral equality in presidential elections.

"One person, one vote—that's the most basic concept there is," he continued. "If you ask any American, he or she will say that's absolutely the way it is. But it's not right now. It's *one person in Rhode Island gets a bigger vote than one person in California.* And if this entire vote rests on tens of thousands of votes in one state, even though Stein won by over five million in the whole country—well, I've been down that road. And this time I'm not leaving it up to the damn Supreme Court to vote for the people who brung 'em to the dance."

"Honey," Flora said, putting her hand on his shoulder, "you're being a real downer."

Virgil smiled. "I suppose you're right. Shall we get jiggy with it?"

All the members of my generation looked at one another blankly.

"After all," Virgil said, "who let the dogs out?"

Dogs? I didn't see any dogs.

"Can't touch this!"

Inexplicably, he started to do this jump 'n' thrump move that must've been real big when he was real small. Flora cranked up the music, and we all started to laugh and move.

The party was saved.

I loved dancing with Jimmy because it was one of the few things I knew that could make him look nervous. He'd grown up in a house where classical dominated. So when everyone started to thrump, it was like Jimmy felt like he was part of a different playlist. He went looking for the notes instead of letting them permeate.

I led. I marauded my hands down his body, then flung myself around him. I could hear Mandy and Janna whooping to my left with Mira in the middle, and could see Virgil and Flora admiring us while they took things a beat or two slower.

After a few songs of this, I needed a quick bathroom break. The downstairs bathroom was occupied, so I skipped up the stairs to where the bedrooms of the house used to be. I usually kept to the downstairs area, so I wasn't as familiar with upstairs as I could have been. The first door I opened was a linen closet. The next was the executive office. I realized my mistake immediately and was quietly closing the door when I noticed two figures in the back of the room, silhouetted against the window shade by a streetlamp outside. Keisha and Sara. Which wouldn't have been out of the ordinary—Keisha was one of Sara's best volunteers—but when my eyes adjusted a little I could see that Sara's hand was under Keisha's shirt, and Keisha was leaning into it like a cat being petted, purring from the joy of it. They were so wrapped up in each other that they didn't see me. Since I hadn't turned the hallway light on, only a gray shade of dimness came into the room with me. I was so surprised, I nearly cried out. But luckily something deeper than surprise took hold of me, and I managed to leave the room without a sound, closing the door before I attracted any notice.

Keisha and Sara? And with Mira right downstairs.

I almost wanted to open the door again, to make sure what I'd seen was true. That it wasn't just a trick of the light that caused Sara's hand to rub against Keisha's body that way. That it wasn't Keisha at all, only some other girl who looked like her.

But of course I didn't open the door again. I stood in the hallway for too long, paralyzed by hundreds of thoughts that didn't add up to a single understanding. Then I finally found my way to the bathroom. I turned on the light and stared at my reflection in the medicine-cabinet mirror. I looked messed up, shocked. Which was a very accurate reflection.

Keisha and Mira, two years older than us, had always been the couple that Jimmy and I wanted to be. They seemed entirely at ease with their love, comfortable enough to argue without ever fighting. They believed they were meant to be together, and we all believed it, too. Because their happiness, their comfort, always spilled over to us. Their light was something we could all read by.

"Keisha and Sara." I said it out loud. As if someone would peek their head out from the shower and say, *Don't be ridiculous.* But instead there was only the sound of my voice. And it rang true.

Even my voice had seen.

I didn't want to jump to conclusions, because all the conclusions jumped straight to endings.

I could go back in and confront them.

No.

I could go downstairs and tell Mira.

No.

I could forget it all.

Not possible.

I was so glad they hadn't seen me. And I wished they had seen me, so it wouldn't be up to me.

I had no idea what to do.

eight

"Did you see Keisha up there?" Mira asked as soon as I got back downstairs.

I could tell from their voice: They had no idea. There wasn't a thread of suspicion in the question.

"Know," I said, understanding full well that it would come out as "no." Lying to myself that I wasn't entirely lying.

They believed me, because they didn't think they had any reason not to. I wanted to say, *Go upstairs yourself,* but at that moment I heard footsteps coming down.

Sara.

She had a big smile for me.

"Welcome to the victory party, Duncan!" she said. There wasn't a crack in her cheer, not a scruple out of place in her expression.

"I've got to find Jimmy," I replied. What I really meant was: *I've got to get away from you right now.*

It must have shown. Even if Mira and Sara couldn't see it, Jimmy could.

"What's going on?" he asked when I got to him.

"Nothing," I said. Then, when he didn't look satisfied with that answer, I nodded toward the open screen and said, "Kansas."

The newsreader cut to a live news conference at the opponent's headquarters.

We turned up the volume.

"Ladies and gentlemen, the good people of America, believers in democracy and defenders of freedom everywhere, I address you tonight because over the past twelve hours a good number of events have come to light in the state of Kansas that have given me clear and fair reason to believe that the election for the next President of the United States is not yet over. Because of this new and important information, I will not concede the election, and will call upon my opponent to refrain from declaring an end to this contest until all the American people, including the good and honest people of Kansas, have had their rightful say. Grave and serious doubts about the election have been raised, and when they are answered, I expect both the truth and the facts will show that I have won the state of Kansas, and thus the Presidency, a sacred office to which I pledge my undying devotion and loyalty. Whether it takes ten more hours, ten more days, or ten more weeks to determine the true and fair winner of this most important contest, I will remain

strong and steadfast until that truth is revealed. May the great
God shine on America, and may freedom ring forever and ever,
amen."

"The man always uses twenty words when two will do!"
Virgil burst out.

The dancing had stopped now. We all watched as Stein
took the podium at his own headquarters.

"He doesn't look that happy," Jimmy mumbled to me.

He was right. Stein looked like he'd been through a tornado, with pieces of his house still in his hair.

"This can't be good," Janna murmured.

As soon as Stein got to the microphone and the reporters
quieted down, he went right to the point.

"What is happening in Kansas is politics as usual, and it's
not good politics. We have won Kansas fair and square, and
we are not going to be bullied or intimidated into losing a state
that we won. The American people have spoken, and five mil-
lion more of them voted for me than voted for my opponent. In
Kansas, seventy-six thousand more of them voted for me than
voted for my opponent. These are the facts, and we will let them
guide us. We will not let rogue members of my opponent's party
throw the election. A democratic nation cannot tolerate that."

*

It was an amazing thing to watch: The more Stein spoke, the more the fire in him blazed. Even if he'd started out weary, each word seemed to energize him. It made me believe in him once more.

But the truth was: It wasn't over. We had thought it was over. We had thought we'd won. But the fight had only intensified.

Sensing this, Virgil turned off the screen and stood in front of it. Sara moved to his side. I looked back and saw that Keisha had returned to the room. I avoided her gaze, because I knew if I caught it, she'd see I was unable to look her in the eye.

"Well, folks, it's looking like our victory party was a little premature," Virgil told us. "But whatever's thrown our way, we can take it. If we've gotta fight for our right, so be it. Wherever we have to take a stand, we'll take a stand. Because those bastards aren't going to take the Presidency away from us. No amount of fear they throw our way is going to do that. Am I right?"

We all nodded.

"What's that?" Virgil wasn't pleased. "I don't think I heard you. Let's try this again. Am I right?"

"Yes!" we called out.

"And are you with me?"

"Yes!"

"Pump up the jam a little more, kids. Are you with me?"

"YES!"

Virgil nodded. "That's more like it."

I looked at the blank screen behind him. That seemed as good an image as any to show how we felt—we weren't sure where we were, or what we were supposed to do, or even what was going on. I knew we were supposed to feel rallied, but mostly I felt confused. Let down, even. Like we'd just run a marathon and were now being told they'd added a twenty-seventh mile. And a twenty-eighth. And maybe even more after that.

If this made me depressed, it made Jimmy angry. He just kept shaking his head, cursing.

"This can't be happening," he said.

I felt a tap on my shoulder. I turned and found Mira and Keisha, holding hands.

"What now?" Mira asked.

I couldn't stop looking at how casually together the two of them were.

"Duncan?" Keisha asked.

I saw you, I wanted to say. But not with Mira there.

"I've gotta go," I said instead.

"I'm with you," Jimmy said. "Let's walk to mine."

We distributed our good-byes. Virgil and Sara told us they'd let us know as soon as they found out what the next steps were. Flora gave us each another big hug. Then we were out in the night, the conversations of the house fading behind us.

Nothing felt right.

nine

It was about a twenty-minute walk to Jimmy's house, and we were silent for the first ten. I kept flashing back to Sara and Keisha, and then to the oblivious look on Mira's face. And I kept seeing Stein before he started talking, and I wondered which was the truth—his expression then or the energy he gave us when he was speaking. Did he secretly think it was over? Would the opposition manage to tip us onto unfair ground?

Jimmy took my hand, and I had to chase out the image of Mira and Keisha holding hands just like us.

Finally Jimmy said, "It's just too much." And at first I thought he was talking about Mira and Keisha. Then I realized, of course, he had no idea. And I didn't want to tell him, because there wasn't anything he could do, either. Telling him would just make him feel as bad as I felt, and I didn't see any reason for that. I would just have to hold on to it myself.

"So close and yet so far," I agreed.

"We can't let it happen."

He lifted his fingers out of mine and started to rub my arm. I pressed in a little more. His touch was nice. Very nice.

We started to kiss, right there on the sidewalk. Not light pecks or sweetheart affections. No—this was need and this was desire and this was our way of trying to negate all the negativity around us. This was what the opposition always wanted to stop, so we did it and did it and did it.

"Can I come over?" I asked.

"Absolutely," he said.

And although we didn't run, we walked faster than before. Because we knew what was next. We let our anticipation block everything else out.

I had been the hesitant one at first, and he hadn't pushed. He wanted me to be ready, and I used that word as my guide—I was waiting for the word *ready* to fit how I felt.

In the beginning, I couldn't get the questions out of my head when we made out. *Am I doing this right? Should I take off my shirt or should I wait for him to do it? How fast is too fast? What if I finish before he does?* I would echo his movements, because that seemed safe. I enjoyed the kissing the most, because sometimes it would be the slowest, most quieting thing, the most intense kind of breathing.

Then I started to let my hands feel, to let my skin react.

He would joke with me, and I'd relax. He'd whisper out-of-the-blue song lyrics in my ear. He'd ask me what I liked and tell me what he liked. I found myself developing a memory of such things. I learned his body, his rhythm, his flutter, his gasp. And slowly all my unspoken questions were answered, and I found myself enjoying it all. I found myself ready.

The first time, he tried to plan it. The right music, the soft sheets, the flowers by the bed. But the way it worked out, the music stopped halfway through, the sheets got pushed to the floor, and the flowers ended up falling on the clock. It was slow, then fast, then slow, then fast, and it was safe in so many more ways than one. It was closeness not because he was inside me but because of what it meant, what we meant, what we could do. It was so intense and so much ours, and once it started we weren't going to stop. Sex wasn't the full extent of our love, but our love was what made it so powerful. It was a new way of getting to know each other. Sometimes we would talk through it, and other times most of the words were knocked away and all my thoughts would form in one-word flashes—

Yes.

Wait.

Me.

There.

Mmm.

Yes.

Turn.

You.

Breathe.

Grasp.

Sweat.

Yes.

Over.

Lower.

More.

Slow.

Yes.

Y e s.

Now.

I loved being naked with him. I loved watching him when his eyes were closed, when he lost control, when he let go and let me take him. I loved when my whole body felt a part of it, when I would grasp and glide and press without having to think about it. When I let go and let my body take me.

And still, what I loved the most was the heartbeating. The heartbeating through kisses. The heartbeating through touch. The sharp, deep heartbeating when I came and the loose, lazy heartbeating of lying there after, drifting in that love-sewn quiet of lying next to him, the gentle return.

This time, we knew Jimmy's parents were out until at least ten. We knew we had the house to ourselves. We could have talked more about the day. We could have turned on the news. But instead we slammed into each other as soon as the door was closed, dropping our book bags, shedding our jackets, stumbling to his room in between mad kisses, kicking off our shoes, pulling off each other's shirts, unbuckling our belts, sliding off our pants, pausing for that awkward moment of sock removal, then wrestling into bed, our underwear the thinnest barrier, soon shed. It wasn't like it had ever been before—we were saying too many things at once. This wasn't want, this was need. We were colliding our way to comfort, shouting with our bodies, pulling ourselves close closer closer. I was pinning him against the mattress and he was leaning up to match my kiss with his, and I was rolling over and he was pressing our bodies together, toe to head, and we were sweating and I was ready and he was ready and we were both so ready for everything in the world to fall into place, just once, just now. I arched my back and he licked my neck. I grabbed him tighter and he pulled at my hair. I was all feeling, and none of those feelings were fear. It felt like war, but I was rooting for both sides.

This was what they were afraid of. But I wouldn't be afraid. I wouldn't.

We stopped to be safe, then continued our push and pull until we got to the rush and then the afterwards. Lying there, I could feel my heartbeat decelerating, calming. I leaned my head on his shoulder and slowly stroked the small canyon of hair down the middle of his chest. Even in the half-light of his nighttime bedroom, I admired the ghost hairs on his neck as he let his hand fall on my leg, his skin three hues darker and one degree warmer than mine.

We stayed like this for as long as we could. This was the closest to sleep that waking could be, and I almost crossed the border. But then Jimmy asked me a question, and his voice was full of such unexpected vulnerability that I felt the full weight of my love for him . . . and wasn't afraid of it, either.

"It's all going to be okay, isn't it?" he asked.

And I responded by holding him close and saying that whatever it took, we would make it okay.

ten

The next two days were like watching a car wreck about to happen and not having any way to stop it.

The governor of Kansas's plan to throw the election to Stein's opponent by disqualifying as many Stein votes as possible soon became clear. Among the groups he was targeting were:

(a) Urban voters whose polling places had stayed open past the election deadline because lines had been so long, even after the board of elections had announced that they were closed.

(b) College voters who, the governor alleged, might have voted twice by using absentee ballots in their home states.

(c) Provisional voters whose identities, he said, had been confirmed "too quickly."

It was a playbook that had been used enough times during the reign of fear that nobody was particularly surprised by it. Virgil was already organizing a campaign to galvanize voters in our state to make it clear they were ready to protest any move the Kansas governor made. Virgil insisted that none of us skip school in order to help, so we had to wait until the last bell rang to head over to headquarters. I tried not to bristle every time Keisha and Sara were out of the room together, but I couldn't help it—I was suspicious of their every move.

I would ask Mira where Keisha had gone to, and they would tell me Keisha and Sara had just run to the store for more envelopes, or that she was in the kitchen making coffee.

I avoided the second floor.

School, however, couldn't be avoided. At school, we were all at one another's throats.

Two days after the election—the morning after Kansas was put back into play—Janna and I walked in to find Mary Catherine leading a prayer circle that walked through hallways, chanting. With a loudness we hadn't known she still possessed, she was beseeching the Lord to swing Kansas to Stein's opponent. The few people in her flock shouted their assent, while the rest of the students just wanted them to get out of the way.

Janna looked pissed.

"I prayed last night, too," she said to me, glaring in Mary Catherine's direction. "I prayed for a good long time to God to do the right thing in Kansas. That's all I said—the right thing. And I guess that's the difference between Mary Catherine and me: I don't feel I need to tell the Lord what the right thing is. I have faith the Lord knows."

Jesse Marin was predictably harsh to me in homeroom. "You're going down," he taunted.

I ignored him and made sure my seat was in place after the pledge.

When we got to Mr. Davis's room, we found Principal Cotter in the back, which actually made me feel a little better. I wondered if Ms. Kaye or some other teachers had talked to him. Whatever the case, Mr. Davis could barely contain his annoyance at being observed. He spat out facts about the War of 1812 like he resented each and every one of them. I kept my head down, because every time Mr. Davis looked my way I could feel his disgust. He wouldn't even turn in Jimmy's direction . . . until Jimmy took off his sweater.

It was warm in the room; it made sense for Jimmy to remove the sweater. Principal Cotter couldn't really argue that he was being provocative. But the motion got Mr. Davis's attention. Midsentence, he saw Jimmy . . . and Jimmy's shirt.

It was simple, really: a white T-shirt with a small American flag in the center. That's it.

But it tripped Mr. Davis up. It gnashed him.

That was the thing about the Decents—they were as possessive of the flag as they were of the country. They thought it should only belong to some people, the *deserving* people. When the whole point of the flag—and the country—was that it belonged to everyone.

While Mr. Davis was clearly surprised to see the flag on Jimmy's T-shirt, I wasn't. I knew that he believed in America, in the same way that Stein believed in America. Not because of what it had been, but because of what it could be. I knew the flag to him was a way of translating a concept made of so many words and understandings and complications into one clear image, the same way you can express love with a single drawn heart. By wearing the flag, he wasn't just saying, *This is mine, too.* He was saying, *This is all of ours.*

Mr. Davis started bombarding him with questions about British troop movements—each of which he answered correctly. Then Mr. Davis moved—as all lessons about the War of 1812 seemingly do—to "The Star-Spangled Banner."

"Our national anthem," Mr. Davis invoked. As if we didn't know.

Jimmy raised his hand.

I was afraid he was going to point out that "The Star-Spangled Banner" hadn't been written as a national anthem, and in fact had been set by Francis Scott Key to the tune of a British drinking song. Mr. Davis clearly didn't want to take any chances—he ignored Jimmy's hand and kept lecturing.

"Ahem," Mira coughed, looking at Jimmy. I got what they were trying to do. I turned to Jimmy, too, as did a large part of the class. Even the ones who hadn't left with us the previous day were playing along. They wanted to see what would happen.

"Mr. Davis," Principal Cotter said, "I believe you have a question."

"Yes, Mr. Jones? What brilliant words do you have to share with us about 'The Star-Spangled Banner'?"

"I just find it interesting that we only kept the first verse," Jimmy said. "I mean, for the national anthem. There were three other verses, right? And the one we made into our national anthem is the one that has all the questions."

"What do you mean, questions?"

"I mean, we don't really know if the flag is still there."

Mr. Davis huffed. "Of course it's still there. Clearly you haven't done your reading—Francis Scott Key woke up early on the morning of September fourteenth, 1814, and saw the flag flying over Fort McHenry to mark victory over the British."

"I know that," Jimmy answered calmly. "What I'm saying is, the national anthem is a question. It doesn't say, ''Tis the star-spangled banner / O long may it wave / O'er the land of the free and the home of the brave'—that's the end of Key's *second* verse. No, instead we use the verse that goes, 'O say does that star-spangled banner yet wave / O'er the land of the free and the home of the brave?' Our national anthem ends with a question mark."

"There is no question," Mr. Davis insisted.

"But there is. That's why it's such a brilliant national anthem—because it asks us to believe the flag is still there, even though there's no way to know for sure."

I knew Jimmy was pushing Mr. Davis closer and closer to the edge. This time, I decided to do something: I started clapping. Keisha, Mira, and some of the others joined in.

"Enough!" Mr. Davis yelled.

"Okay, quiet," Principal Cotter chimed in. But Mr. Davis was already long past that.

"Shut up! All of you! Shut up!" he shouted. Then he turned on Jimmy. "How dare you come into my class and talk like that?"

"I dare because my country allows me to," Jimmy replied.

Principal Cotter was on his feet now.

"Everybody quiet here," he said. "Let's focus on the lesson and not turn this into politics, okay? This is a history class, not a rally."

But why else do we learn history? I wanted to ask. *And don't you realize that silence itself is politics?*

Mr. Davis still seethed.

"Teach," Principal Cotter told him.

He went back to troop movements and the Madisons fleeing the White House. I don't think I'd ever paid more attention to him; the edge was keeping me awake.

In the hallway after class, I took Jimmy's hand and said, "Nice shirt."

"Tell that to Kansas," he replied glumly. Then he smiled at me and said, "Thanks for the applause. That was a nice touch. I'm sure Mr. Davis will be complaining to all his QAnon cronies about it, saying it's clearly the space lasers that made you do it."

"Jewish space lasers," I said. "Queer Jewish space lasers, brainwashing us all into thinking for ourselves."

Most teachers didn't want students checking phones in class, so we had to keep up with the news between periods and at lunch. As the threat in Kansas became more and more real, an angry sadness settled in my gut. Jesse and his crew became bolder in their assurance. Mandy and Janna tried to make us optimistic, and Gus refused to believe that the election would be thrown.

Then, after lunch, something wrong happened. Jimmy and I were at my locker, switching books. One of his fingers was in one of my belt loops, just casually there. We were talking about going to headquarters that night when we heard it, that one word:

"Fags."

It was Satch who'd said it, with Jesse and this other guy Rand next to him.

"What?" Jimmy said, letting his finger fall from my jeans, turning to face the insult. "What did you say?"

"You heard me," Satch said, like he was proud of it.

I was totally thrown. That word had never been shot at me before, especially not in school by someone I knew. It was such a Decent thing to do, to act like it was their God-given right to be hurtful to someone else. It felt like hate, and it felt personal.

I would've stayed paralyzed. But not Jimmy. He was immediately staring Satch down.

"What're you saying, Satch?" he said. "Don't hold back now."

I looked at Jesse, and I have to admit that even he seemed a little surprised. But he wasn't going to let his friend down.

"Get off, Jimmy," he said.

"No, I want to see if Satch is done. Because I can think of plenty of other insults he can hurl my way. Where you want to go next with this, Satch? You probably noticed that as well as being gay, I'm also not white. Perhaps that bothers you, too?"

He was right in Satch's face, only a few inches between them. Satch shoved him away. Jimmy shoved back.

There were other people in the hall now. Watching. Letting it play out.

"Just take your fag President wannabe and get the hell out of here," Satch said. Then he went to shove Jimmy again, and a number of things happened at once:

Jimmy knocked Satch's arm before Satch could knock Jimmy.

Jesse and I both jumped in to stop it.

Satch spun back, striking out.

Jesse and I almost collided. To avoid Jesse, I moved a little to the right—

—and got hit right in the face by Satch's elbow.

So I ended up being the one knocked over, my eye bruised. Jesse and Rand pulled Satch back. Jimmy bent down to see if I was okay.

It all happened so fast. All unleashed by a single hateful word.

"Are you okay?" Jimmy asked. I nodded . . . even though I was holding my eye.

"Never been better," I said.

"It hurts?"

"Yeah, it hurts."

I didn't want to go to the nurse's office. (I could hear her: *"You?!? In a fight?!?"*) So Jimmy got a bag of ice from the cafeteria and we sat out back for sixth period.

"This is getting out of control," I said.

He didn't disagree.

People have to learn their hate from somewhere. I used to think it was always from their parents, or somewhere at home. But when a whole political party decides to gain votes by giving people permission to indulge in their deepest hatreds, so intimately tied to their deeper fears, I have to imagine that what you hear at home is only part of it.

Their pride was tied to making us feel ashamed. Our pride had to be stronger than that.

Word spread that Stein was going to make a big announcement in a press conference at eight o'clock.

We all waited in nervous anticipation at headquarters that night. My eye—not quite a black eye, but still a little purple—was the object of a lot of scrutiny and concern. I didn't like the attention and would have been able to shrug it off if Jimmy hadn't been beside me the whole time, watching over me and telling people what had happened. I knew he felt bad, and I'd told him more than once that it wasn't his fault. I couldn't even give Satch full blame for the blow, since I didn't think he'd expected my face to be anywhere near his elbow. Still, I resented the chain of events that had led to the collision, and the fact that Satch hadn't said sorry after.

Virgil shook his head when he saw it, and Flora insisted on running upstairs for some ointment. Sara was nowhere to be seen, which might have explained why Mira and Keisha appeared inseparable again. I wondered how genuine that was, and hated myself for thinking that way.

Finally, it was eight o'clock. We all quieted down and watched the screen. As reporters scrambled for position, Stein walked up to the podium at his national headquarters and began to speak.

"My fellow Americans, the time has come for us to do something about Kansas. A small group of politically motivated people are trying to disenfranchise, manipulate, and lie their way to winning this election. Although they say it is being done in the name of fairness, it is truly being done out of greed and self-interest. We cannot let it happen. This afternoon, I received independent verification of something I already believed to be

true: My campaign has won the majority of votes in the state of Kansas. This cannot be denied, and the fact that it is being denied must be viewed as a call to action.

"I'll be honest with you: This is not something I say lightly. It would be easy for me to remain silent, to leave the fate of this nation in the hands of two teams of lawyers, and ultimately the courts. But that isn't what this country is about, and it isn't what I'm about. You deserve the truth, and we all must fight for it if we must.

"I ask my opponent to concede this election and abide by the independent commission led by former governor Hopkins, which states clearly and unequivocally that the election results in Kansas are correct as initially reported. Any attempt by the current governor to invalidate these results should be stopped immediately. This is not an election that can be tampered with or questioned. The people have spoken, and now they must be heard. To do otherwise is against everything this country is about. America cannot and will not abide dishonesty, untruths, or the cynical manipulation of the voting process. Our values are much, much stronger than that."

At a separate news conference, the former governor—a member of the opposition party—verified that his commission had monitored the voting in Kansas, had checked the results, and was satisfied beyond doubt that Stein's margin of victory was accurate.

Then more troubling news began to come in: A Kansas

election official told a reporter that she had been asked to erase some votes from the electronic polling machine in her district. Another person, a college student, volunteered that his name had been on the current governor's "double-voting" list, proclaimed that he had not filled out an absentee ballot for his home state, and said that if one was discovered, it would be a forgery sent in by someone other than him as a way of disqualifying his vote. The opposition party, he said, could easily obtain students' home addresses to pull such a stunt.

The opposition candidate held his own press conference, refusing to concede, saying that God wanted him to see this thing through to the end, through any channels and means necessary.

Finally, around eleven o'clock our time, Stein stepped in front of the cameras again.

"I can see which way the wind is being blown in Kansas. And the only way to stop it is to blow back harder. We must let the truth fill our lungs, our purpose fill our hearts and make us strong.

"This is what I say:

"I am going to Kansas.

"And this is what I ask:

"I want you, the American people, the ones who elected me as your next President, to come to Kansas, too. I want you there beside me to prevent an injustice from occurring. I want our

opponents to see the faces of all the people they are trying to deceive. I want them to know they will not get away with it.

"Come to Kansas.

"I know this is asking a lot. I know it has never before been asked in these circumstances. But in times of trial, as we have done so often in the past, we must come together as a community. We must be our best selves. We must do what's right.

"You have made your voice heard by voting for me. Do not let your voice be taken away.

"Ensure democracy.

"Come to Kansas."

eleven

"Let's go!" Gus called out.

Sara came running into the room, explaining that she'd been on the phone with someone at national headquarters who said that there was going to be a rally in front of the Kansas statehouse on Sunday afternoon.

"That gives us two and a half days to get there," another college volunteer, Joe, said.

"How long a drive can it be?" Gus asked. "No more than a day and a half."

"I don't think we can all fit in your Prius," Jimmy pointed out. "Not for that amount of time."

"No hindrance," Gus said. "I'm sure I can borrow the church van."

"No need for that," Virgil said. "Flora's son, Clive, has a bus."

There didn't seem any doubt that we'd soon be on our

way. Virgil wanted us all to go to school on Friday, but we'd head off right after.

"Finally we can do something," Jimmy said, and I guess that summed up a large part of what we were all feeling.

If Stein needed us, we would go.

"Come to Kansas," his voice kept saying on the news. They couldn't stop showing it.

The opposition candidate clearly hadn't anticipated Stein's speech. At first, all he said was "Don't come to Kansas." It took another day for him to ask his supporters to come to Kansas, too.

"This isn't going to be a vacation," Virgil warned us. "Don't think it's going to be easy."

On the way home, I listened to some of the commentators commentating. One of them harkened back to the Civil War.

"It's Bleeding Kansas all over again," he said.

I didn't know what he meant. Luckily the host didn't know, either, so the commentator explained, "Kansas was founded by abolitionists who wanted to prevent slavery from spreading from Missouri. They put their lives on the line for it, and when Missouri invaded to stop the Kansas opposition, it became Bleeding Kansas.

"The same passions," he went on to say, "exist here."

It was after midnight when I walked in my front door. I knew my parents would probably still be up, but I wasn't expecting them to be waiting in the den for me to come home.

"Where've you been, Duncan?" my father asked.

"At Stein headquarters, with Jimmy and the others," I answered. "You knew that."

"It's a school night."

"Sorry."

I didn't sound sorry, and he knew it. I started to climb the stairs, but then he said, "Come back down here." I did, and when he told me to sit down, I did that, too.

My parents had never really been cool parents, but they hadn't been uncool, either. They were just there, and I loved them, and they loved me, and we didn't really understand one another at all. I think it had always been clear to them that I was gay, and that hadn't been much of a problem. When I'd first started dating Jimmy, I'd hesitated a little before bringing him home—not because I was afraid of how they'd react, but more because I liked the idea of keeping my world with him separate from my world with them. When I'd become involved with the Stein campaign, they'd been supportive without being encouraging; as Jews, they were convinced a Jewish candidate would never win, and my father never really bought into the possibility of the Great Community the same way that I did. I was pretty sure they'd both voted for Stein, but they didn't want to make a big deal about it.

So I was surprised-but-not-completely-surprised when they sat me down and told me I wasn't going to Kansas.

"What do you mean?" I asked.

"I'm sure you saw Stein tonight," my father said. "And I'm sure you and your friends are all ready to go to Kansas to take a stand. When you're older and more mature you'll be able to do such things, if you still want to. But right now you're only sixteen and you're not going to throw yourself into such a volatile situation."

I could see my mother staring at my not-black-but-kind-of-purple eye. I wanted to cover it, but it was too late.

"What happened to you?" she asked, concerned.

"Nothing. Stupid accident," I said.

"Oh, honey. Did you put ice on it?"

"Yes."

"Do you want more?"

"I'm okay."

I realized I was getting distracted from the argument I needed to be making.

"Look," I said, "I *am* going to Kansas. Flora's son, Clive, has a bus, and we're all going to go together. Not just kids, but adults, too. It'll be fine. I promise."

"I don't think you're hearing me, Duncan," my father said. "You're not going. You're staying here."

I don't think you're *hearing* me, I wanted to say. But I knew that wouldn't go over well.

"Is that understood?" he prompted.

"Duncan," my mother said, her voice gentler than my father's, "I think we need to explain. We've always been proud of you for all the work you've done for Stein and the dedication that you've shown." *This* was a surprise. I must have looked at her with complete disbelief, because she laughed and said, "Don't look so shocked. You know I'm not the type to get involved, but that doesn't mean I can't be proud of my son for getting involved. We haven't minded when you've come home late, when you've gone into some dangerous neighborhoods to talk to strangers, even when you've cut school—yes, we know about that, and we're trusting you not to make it a habit. You seem to forget that your attendance record is online for us to see.

"But this is different, honey. You're going to want to think that we're making you stay here for some political reason. You'll want to think of us as the enemy. But honestly, it's not that. It's because we're your parents and we want you to be safe. You can't possibly remember what the riots were like. You can't possibly know how these things can go wrong and become violent. Stein wants you to come to Kansas—fine. But he can't guarantee that things will remain peaceful. I know he wants them to be. Believe me, Dunc, I know. But this isn't some picnic. This is a fight—he says so himself—and when you join a fight, you can get really, really hurt. Especially in this country. Especially right now, when everyone is so divided. So that's why I—we—want you to stay here."

She didn't say *Look at your eye,* but she didn't have to. I thought of a thousand Satches and Jesses heading to Kansas—and millions of the people who'd yelled at me on the phone, who'd been so ready to scald Stein supporters with the sheer will of their despising.

"There must be something you can do here at home," my mother went on. "I'll even help you. If you want. You just can't go to Kansas."

I went to my room more confused than ever. Because I hadn't really been thinking about what would happen when we got to Kansas—I'd been caught up in the excitement of going, of being part of the team, of being on a mission with Jimmy. Maybe none of us had really thought it through. Because what if we were really heading toward another Bleeding Kansas? What if the opponent's supporters were ready to do anything to throw the election?

I wondered if Stein himself had thought it through. How many people did he really think would come? Was it just a big publicity stunt? Would it spiral out of control?

I pictured millions of people angrily calling me a fag or a dirty Jew. I imagined crowds and crowds of people overwhelming me. I saw myself losing Jimmy, losing everyone I knew. Riot police pressing in. Gas in the air. Being pushed and grabbed and yelled at.

It wasn't a nightmare; I wasn't asleep yet. I was seeing it.

I didn't want to face it. Not the hostility. Not the chance of my parents being right.

I really had believed I was going to Kansas.

And now I was starting to realize I wasn't going after all.

twelve

I thought I might change my mind about changing my mind. But if anything, the next morning's news seemed to support my parents' position. The opposition was now saying that if Stein's supporters were going to Kansas in large numbers, then his supporters would "take no prisoners." The governor was calling in the National Guard. The current President was said to be "reviewing the situation." Already flights were full. Rent-a-cars were scarce. The people of Kansas were preparing for an invasion of outsiders, whether they liked it or not.

I didn't know what I was going to say to Jimmy. So I fell quiet. He misunderstood and thought I was still bothered by the run-in with Satch the previous day. For their part, Satch and Jesse kept their distance. School almost appeared normal. Word spread that Mary Catherine and her parents had already left for Topeka.

I started to pay attention not just to the kids who were talking about the election but also to the kids who weren't talking about it at all. I'd ignored them for the past two days, but now I was feeling almost jealous. Whether or not Stein would be President didn't appear to matter to them; they cared about their field hockey game after school or whether the boy they liked would like them back or whether they'd be able to get their homework done before it was collected during third period. The election was enough to get their attention for a day—maybe. After that, it was back to life.

I asked myself why I had to care so much. Then I reminded myself how vulnerable I was. I didn't want being queer or being Jewish to mean being defined by my vulnerability, by the long history of hate and injustice being directed against us. I didn't think any of the opposition politicians were as bad as Hitler; but I also knew that a gay Jew in Berlin in 1930 wouldn't have thought Hitler was as bad as Hitler, either. Like so many other nonwhite or nonstraight or non-Christian people in America, an element of my pride *had* to be vigilance. Ignorance wasn't a luxury that our history could afford.

But if that was the case—if I had to be vigilant—why wasn't I going to Kansas?

Or did vigilance require me to understand that going there meant too much risk?

At lunch, Gus was talking about music for the bus and Keisha was talking about sleeping arrangements and Jimmy was saying they had to remember to bring poster paper and markers with them, because all banner-making supplies were probably sold out in Kansas. Janna mentioned bringing candles for Jimmy's birthday on Monday, and I double-gulped. Everyone's bags, it seemed, were already packed.

"How were your parents?" Jimmy finally asked me.

"Not good," I said.

But he didn't ask the natural follow-up question, assuming I'd managed to make my way past them.

We were supposed to meet at headquarters at five. It wasn't until three that I told him. We were walking to my house, I guess to pick up my bags.

"Look," I finally had the guts to say, "I don't think I'm going to be able to go."

"Very funny," Jimmy said, and kept walking.

I stopped and pulled at his shirt. "No. Really. No blinking this time."

"What are you talking about?"

He was looking at me with such annoyed confusion, his sweet dark eyes narrowing.

"I can't go. My parents said I can't."

Now I really had his attention.

"You really aren't joking, are you?" he said.

"I'm really not joking."

"But we're doing this together. We've always done this together."

"I know. But I can't do this part."

I knew what was coming next.

Deep breath. Look to the ground, then back in my eyes. "And you waited until now to tell me?"

"I just—I don't know." What could I say? I knew he was going to think less of me, but I'd hoped to minimize the lessness.

"What?" He wanted me to tell him something, anything that made sense, even though it was clear in his voice that he doubted there could be any such explanation. At the very least, he wanted me to acknowledge that.

But all I could come up with was a repeat performance of "I don't know."

He sighed. "This is so typical, Duncan."

Which was what I was afraid of. Making the lessness part of a pattern.

"What do you mean?" I asked.

"Are you kidding? We're supposed to leave in, what, two hours? And you're backing out?"

"Well, it's not like it's been planned for weeks. . . ."

"So what did they say to you? Why can't you go?"

"They just don't think it's a good idea."

"Oh. That's a *great* reason."

Scorn. I'd hit the vein of scorn.

"Don't get angry with me, okay?" I implored. "They just think it's—I don't know—dangerous or something."

I thought he'd try to argue that point. Say it wasn't dangerous at all. But instead he said, "So?"

"What do you mean, so?"

"I mean, of course it's a little dangerous. But staying

here and doing nothing is more dangerous. You know that, Duncan."

"I know. But, really, I can't."

There was sadness in his eyes as well as anger. "Can't, Duncan? Or won't?"

"What do you mean?"

"You know what I mean."

"No, I don't."

We both knew I did.

"Look, do you really want me to say it?"

I couldn't believe we were plummeting into this conversation. This wasn't at all where I wanted to be or what I wanted us to be saying. But I couldn't get us anywhere else.

"Well, now you have to," I told him, for the first time letting some of my own annoyance out. "Don't you?"

"Don't snap at me. *I'm* not the one backing out."

I was totally open to him. Totally vulnerable. And because of that, I couldn't stand that he was so critical of me.

"Is that what I'm doing?" I said.

"Looks like it, doesn't it? And you're doing it because you're afraid."

"That's not it."

"C'mon, Duncan," he said, almost tenderly, like I was a good ten years younger than him. "You have to take a little risk and you want to run in the other direction."

"You make it sound like that's what I always do."

"I'm not saying that."

"Well, that's not fair."

"I'm just saying . . ."

"Yes?"

"You're afraid. Of your parents. Of what might happen."

It was like this rip was occurring, because we were each pulling in a different direction and couldn't stop.

"I'm not afraid of my parents," I told him.

"So it's not about them, is it?"

"Look—" *Please stop,* I wanted to say. *Please can we stop?*

"Yes?"

And *Please can we stop?* came out as "Why are you doing this?"

This did not go over well.

"Why am *I* doing this? You mean, why am I disappointed that my boyfriend is backing out of what could be the most important trip of our lives? I don't know . . . could it be because my boyfriend is backing out of what could be the most important trip of our lives?"

"So you're saying if I don't show up, the governor of Kansas is going to say, 'Hey, I guess we can throw the election now—Duncan's not here.' But if I go, he'll give in. Is my presence really *that* important?"

"It should be that important *to you.* That's what I'm saying."

"Well, I'm sorry I can't be you."

Rip.

"What does that mean?"

Rip.

"It means, I'm sorry that I actually have to think about

what might happen. That I might not want to go to a random state to be attacked by people who see me as the enemy. That might not be the kind of weekend I want to have."

"Oh, so this is about your weekend plans?"

"That's not what I'm saying, and you know it."

I hadn't lost sight of the fact that I loved him, but I wasn't feeling any of it now. Or I was only feeling that part of love that can be misshaped so easily into anger and sadness and pain. He seemed as impervious as always, and that made it worse.

I knew I was in the wrong. A coward. But at the same time I wanted Jimmy to forgive me for that. I wanted him to let me be who I had to be. I resented that he wouldn't, almost as much as I resented myself for not being able to go with him.

Finally he broke the silence with a simple "Fine."

"Fine?"

"What else do you want me to say? Fine. Don't come. I'll send you some postcards."

"And that's it? You're just going to go to Kansas."

Now Jimmy was officially angry. "What? Do you want me to be afraid and stay home, too? I don't think so."

I closed my eyes, slowed things down, said, "That's not what I meant."

Then I opened my eyes and saw that Jimmy's expression had softened a little, too. "Look," he said, "I had to beg my parents not to come with me on the bus. That's the way my family is—they've always been breaking down walls and doing what they believe in. I guess that's not always the way it goes."

"You know I believe in this, Jimmy."

"I know. But what are you going to do about it? That's the question, isn't it?"

I put my hand on his arm, moved my thumb against his bracelet. "I don't like fighting with you. You know that."

"Believe me," he said, moving his hand to hold my elbow, "I'm not liking this, either."

Okay. This felt better.

"Look," I said tentatively, "maybe I *am* afraid."

"Of what?"

"Of things going wrong. Of it turning into a riot. Of getting hurt. Of failing. Of losing you."

Jimmy shook his head. "You're not going to lose me."

"I don't mean like losing you as a boyfriend. God, I hope not. I mean like losing you in a crowd."

He tightened his grip on my arm. "I won't leave your side."

"But the other things—"

"That's why it's called *taking a stand* instead of just *standing*—there are things trying to stop you from being there, so you have to fight for it. And I don't mean getting into a fight. I mean simply getting there and holding your ground. Millions of us, Duncan. It's going to be millions. Yeah, it won't matter whether or not two of us are there. But how often do you have a chance to be a part of something so powerful?"

The only thing clear to me was that nothing was going to be clear to me. I wasn't going to feel like I should go. And I wasn't going to feel like I should stay. Whichever choice I made, I would regret it. Whichever choice I didn't make, I would regret it.

We walked a little more and arrived at my front yard. Both of my parents were at work.

"Give me an hour," I said.

"To get your stuff ready?"

Jimmy's relief was so obvious that I almost said yes.

But instead I told him, "No, to decide."

He looked at the ground. "Oh. Okay."

"I'm sorry."

"No, really—it's okay."

But I was sorry. To be disappointing him. To be disappointing myself.

I hugged him and he hugged me back.

"Go and decide," he said. "Turn on the news. See what's going on."

thirteen

The question became:
What are you willing to do for something you believe in?

I turned on the news. People were already starting to arrive in Kansas.

Stein was there. Martinez was there. All the congresspeople and senators from their party were flying in for the rally.

The governor again insisted the election had not been decided.

Two more people came forward expressing doubts about the governor's "investigation."

There was a woman from Topeka on the news begging people not to come.

"We're just not ready for this kind of thing," she said.

*

I realized if I wasn't going to go, I had to call Virgil and the others to tell them I wasn't coming.

I didn't want to.

I realized if I was going to go, I had to call at least one of my parents to say I was going.

I didn't want to.

A half hour passed.

I started to pack.

Five minutes later, I stopped packing.

I asked myself:

What would you give to have Stein as President?

Your weekend?

Would you be willing to stand up to your parents?

To people who hated you?

I told myself:

The answer to the last question is yes.

Even if I didn't believe I was the kind of person who

could stand up to the people who hated me, I wanted to be the kind of person who would.

I called my mother.

"I have to go," I said.

There was a long pause on her end of the line. In the background, I could hear people talking and typing.

Finally she said, "I was worried you were going to say that."

"Mom, I—"

"Duncan, let me say my peace. You've put me and your father in an impossible position, and I want to explain it to you. As a mother, the idea of you being there horrifies me. It brings up all these images—students being teargassed by police, insurrectionists raging into our Capitol, the chaos these clashes can unleash. I picture myself sitting on the couch, watching violence unfold, and feeling utterly helpless because I won't know if you are in the midst of it or not. I know there is strength in numbers, and that you're not going to be alone. But all it takes is one person with a gun to turn something peaceful into something deadly. That is a risk I will never, as your mother, be comfortable with. So that is my position as your mother.

"At the same time, as a person who lives in this country, I understand how dangerous it can be to allow power to be stolen from you. I recognize that this is your future at stake, and that maybe if my generation and my parents' generation had stood up more, we wouldn't have had as many deaths and disasters in the past few decades as we've had.

"Ultimately, you are sixteen years old, not six, and your father and I talked most of last night and realize that we can't stand in your way here, even if it means we'll spend the next few days terrified that something is going to happen to you. I talked to Virgil while you were at school, and he assured me you'd be in good hands. He understands my concerns, and I trust him to abide by them."

"So you're saying . . ."

"I'm saying I want your phone on at all times. I want the numbers of everyone else on that bus. I want you to stay out of trouble, do you understand me? If it looks like there's going to be a riot or a fight or even just a rough spot, I want you to get out of there." Then she started crying, just a little. "Sorry," she said. "It's not easy letting you go, you know."

"I know."

"Be sure to pack at least two days' extra underwear and socks."

"I already did."

"And take some food, just in case you get stuck."

"I already did."

"And keep some extra money—"

"—in my toiletry kit. Check."

"I guess you have been paying attention, haven't you?"

"It'll be okay," I told her.

"Go out there and save this election," she said. "Then come right back home."

"Thanks, Mom." That was all I needed to say. The rest—that she would talk to my father, that I would call her every night, that I would take care of myself and try to take care of my country—was all understood.

Before she hung up, she made sure to say she loved me, and I made sure to say I loved her back.

Just before my promised hour was up, I called Jimmy to let him know I was coming. I think part of me was expecting a parade, or at least a firework or two in response. But all he said was "I was hoping that was what you were going to say."

Janna's mom drove Janna and me (and our bags) to Stein headquarters. The bus was outside waiting—clearly Gus had arrived early to decorate it, using the large magnetic letters to spell out some good slogans: THE TRUTH WILL SET US FREE and HAVE FAITH and THIS LAND WAS MADE FOR YOU AND ME. Finally he had written KANSAS WILL NOT FALL.

I looked to find Jimmy as soon as I got there, but Virgil told me he hadn't shown up yet. So I waited, and was perhaps too relieved to see that when Jimmy arrived the first thing he did was look to find me. I ran over and hugged him close, a beat longer than our hugs usually lasted, an extra moment to encompass all the apologies I was feeling and all the doubts I feared he still had.

"You don't make it easy," he murmured to me as we hugged.

"I don't have the ability to make something this hard be easy," I murmured back. "But being with you helps."

We stored our suitcases in the bottom of the bus as Virgil explained that Sara had found us a house to stay in—the best friend of one of her roommates lived in Lawrence, twenty-one miles from the state capitol in Topeka. It was going to be crowded—there were sixteen of us—but sleeping on floors was the least of our worries at this point.

The bus wasn't full—Flora said it was possible we'd pick up more people along the way. Inside, it looked like any old kind of public transportation—the muted seats, the narrow aisle, the windows stained by years of dried rain. But once we were all on board, it felt like something extraordinary. Jimmy sat next to me and I felt like the world was starting to fall back into place, that we all had a purpose and we were all on the road to that purpose.

Before we left, Virgil stood at the front of the bus and told us he wanted to say a few words.

"I wish Stein was here right now to talk to you," he began, "because that man has a way with words that I'll never have. But since he's busy at the moment, you all are left with me. I know you've stopped your lives on twenty-four hours' notice to go on this journey. I have to tell you—I have no idea what's going to happen, or what it's going to be like. You'd think that a man of my age would have some idea. But honest to God, I can't see which way this one's going to go.

"This is what I know, and how I see it as an old Black man who's spent his whole life in this country. I know that Kansas came into existence in part because a number of people were willing to put their lives on the line to defeat slavery. I know that wasn't easy and I know that in the end the right side prevailed. I know that a hundred years after that, a Black girl named Linda Brown and her family fought their way through the courts so Linda could go to a school seven blocks from her home in Topeka—a school that until then had been for whites only. I know that her case went all the way to the Supreme Court and led to the abolition of school segregation in America.

"I know that more recently Kansas has been the home to a lot of people who like to use Jesus's name to be unkind and uncivil to people unlike themselves. But I also know that there were always more people around who stood by Jesus's message of love and kindness. It's been a good forty years since I last went to Kansas, and I imagine it's changed like this country's changed—sometimes for the better and sometimes for the worse. I know that of all the great shifts that have occurred in America—the freedom of the slaves, the rights of women, the equality of gays and lesbians, the Black Lives Matter reckoning, the fight for trans rights— none has happened easily, and certainly none has happened instantly and without serious attacks and backlash. But the reason we have the rights that we have is because the fair-minded people who came before us would not give up.

"In my life, I have seen elections stolen—either outright or through the electoral college. I have seen wars fought for no real reason, and I have seen wars fought because there was no other way to get to peace. I have seen the rich get richer and I have seen the poor get poorer. I have seen facts get harder and harder to hide—and easier and easier to manipulate. I have been angry and I have been frustrated and I have been ecstatic and I have been proven right and wrong and back again. I have given up on some things, but I have refused to give up on most things. And I can honestly say that all of it—*all of it*—seems to have led me to where we are, here and now.

"I'm not saying we're going to change everything. Heck, I don't even know if we're going to change *anything*. But there are moments—either in your own life or the life of the world around you—when an event looks you right in the eye and says: *This is important. What are you going to do?* And our answer—right here, right now—is that we are going to take a stand. We are not going to give up. We are not going to let things happen because we don't want to get involved. We are going to intervene, because it's our right—if not our duty—as citizens to intervene. Justice doesn't triumph because anybody tells it to. It triumphs when we push it and carry it and shout it and embrace it until it triumphs. That's what we're doing here. That's why we're going."

I had never seen Virgil speak so long and so forcefully before, and from the look on his face when he was done, I would've guessed that Virgil had never seen it, either. We all cheered after his final word and continued cheering when Clive closed the door and pulled the bus out onto the highway. Then, slowly, we settled into our seats. We started to get lost in our thoughts. We watched as the sky dimmed and the headlights turned on.

Jimmy leaned against the window, staring out at the blur of cars and roadside. I couldn't tell what he was thinking, nor did I feel comfortable asking. I wanted us to be on this journey together, but in some small way it felt like we were each on our own journey. The best I could do was take mine on the same path as his. The best I could hope was to be by his side as we went along.

I closed my eyes and felt us taken forward.

PART TWO

fourteen

We were driving through the middle of the country in the middle of the night. I'd lost track of place in the same way I'd lost track of time—all I knew was that it was late, and we were on a highway, and I couldn't sleep. Friday night and Saturday day had passed uneventfully as we drove deeper into America. Now it was Saturday night, and I'd almost grown used to the sound of the bus breathing its heat. Everyone else seemed to be asleep, their eyes closed and their screens at rest. I felt a stirring next to me—Jimmy taking a look out of the window, watching all the nowhere-somewhere passing at a headlight pace, his face a shifting map of shadows.

"You up?" I asked gently.

"Yeah," he said, his voice lower with the weight of night-time. "Just thinking."

"What about?" My own voice was a bare whisper, a pencil mark on the air.

"I dunno. Things."

Over the past twenty-four hours, I'd been letting the rips between us heal slowly rather than try to fix them with too many stitches of apology. I relied on the quiet gestures, like putting my hand on his leg now, grounding us together as everything else moved by.

"What kind of things?" I asked.

Silence for a beat. A slight moan from somewhere behind us—dialogue with a bad dream, or the sound of a half-awake stretch. I was fully turned to him now, secretly glad he was awake so I didn't have to take such empty distance alone.

"I think we have to be realistic," he said, measuring out his words as if he were using each one to fill the gap in a puzzle.

"About winning this?" I asked.

"No. About us."

Now he was looking at me head-on, and I didn't know what to do. I didn't know what he meant. I'd always hated the word *realistic*. Or, more truthfully, I'd always hated the way people used the word *realistic*—as if it were a limitation, as if reality were something that conformed so severely to likelihood that surprising things could never, ever happen. From what I'd seen, reality was much more complicated than that. Sometimes it was remarkably predictable, but a lot of the time it didn't go the way anybody would expect. I didn't believe in using probabilities to rule out possibilities.

It wasn't like Jimmy to put so much faith in *realistic*. I thought he knew how little sense reality made. Especially in terms of us.

"Where is this coming from?" I asked now. "We don't want to be realistic. Love isn't realistic."

I could immediately see that it was a mistake to use the word *love*—it didn't make Jimmy any more comfortable with the conversation. But I didn't want to take it back, either, because that would mean something much worse than discomfort.

He put his hand on mine, so I could feel his palm on my skin and his leg underneath my own palm. The warmth there, so familiar.

"It's nothing," he said. "Really. I'm just talking about—I don't know, the long term. I know you don't like to talk about it or think about it . . . but I guess I can't help it. I mean, we're sixteen. I'm almost seventeen. We can't act like this is going to be forever, right?"

"But we can't act like it's not," I insisted. "Why would we do that?"

It's not like I knew for sure that Jimmy and I were going to grow old together—that we were going to still be in love through college and after college and all the years beyond that. It's not like I had our wedding planned and our children ready for their school pictures and the wallpaper for our bedroom picked out. But, sure, I had daydreams. I had hopes, even if I didn't have certainty or even faith. I liked those daydreams. I saw no reason to free myself from them prematurely.

Jimmy didn't argue with me. But he didn't say anything to make it better, either, leaving me to be the one to continue.

"Is this about what happened before we left?" I had to ask. "About me not coming? I told you I was sorry about that."

"It's not that," he said, the sadness so clear across his face, mingled with the lasting tiredness. "I guess I've just been thinking—there are so many things that are bigger than us. There are so many people we haven't met, so many places we've never been. I love you, and I love being with you, and I don't want that to change. But I can't ignore the fact that it might change. Right?"

Did he really want me to tell him he was right? Say, *Yeah, let's be realistic. Let's start to wonder when it's going to end. Let's give in to the odds that we won't be together 'til we die. Let's allow ourselves to give up a little . . . and then watch as that giving up grows and grows and grows until we've given up altogether.*

I couldn't tell him any of that. I would not be the one to lead us down that path.

I leaned over to him, my elbow hitting the button for the reading light above us, sparking its small spotlight halo. Keeping the one hand between his two different touches, I moved my other hand to his cheek, then back to his hair. When I kissed him, I closed my eyes. He wasn't ready for the kiss, but he received it. I pulled back before he could lose his linger.

"That's what I know," I said, my voice still barely above a whisper, my eyes steady.

He smiled a little. Shook his head at me. Thinking it was too simple, but not disputing it.

"I don't want to hurt you," he said. "Ever."

"Then don't."

Another sound came from the back of the bus—this time a *shhhh*.

Jimmy curved himself more into the seat, ready for sleep. I felt, though, that I couldn't let him—not yet. I wanted to erase as much of this conversation as possible before he left me awake.

"I don't want to have to think about this," I told him honestly.

"I know," he said, complete understanding in his voice. "I'm sorry I said it. Really, it isn't anything. I'm just tired. I should never open my mouth after midnight. Especially on a bus."

"The only way to deal with the future is to make sure the present is okay."

He moved his hand from my hand, onto my thigh.

"It is," he said. "I promise. We'll be okay."

He was closing his eyes now. Moving his hand over my thigh, under my shirt, up my skin.

I closed my eyes. Felt him gliding there. Then resting, right on my side, arm around and holding me gently.

His breathing slowed. I opened my eyes and studied his face, watched his chest rise and fall. I'd seen him like this so many times, more in shades of day than shades of night. Napping, sleeping, breathing . . . I felt such tender fascination to see it. I could be his quiet watcher for as long as he was next to me.

Suddenly there was a shout from the back of the bus.

"WHAT THE—?"

Jimmy opened his eyes, pulled back his hand, and we both turned at the same time. There, a few rows behind us, Mira was standing in the aisle, screaming at Keisha and Sara, who had somehow managed to sneak to the back of the bus together, a single blanket covering them both.

"HOW COULD YOU?"

Other people were stirring now, waking.

"I can explain," Keisha said quietly, trying to establish a calmer tone.

"Okay. Explain."

Sara decided to jump in. "We were just—"

"I don't want to hear a single word from you. I want to hear it from her."

But Keisha just started crying.

"Oh my God," Jimmy whispered to me. "Were Keisha and Sara—?"

"Yeah," I told him.

"Are you sure?"

I nodded.

"What?" Mira was yelling now. "WHAT?!?"

Finally there was another person in the aisle—Janna coming to put her hand on Mira's shoulder, to take them back to their seat in the front. Sara stood up—both she and Keisha had been clothed under the blanket—saying it wasn't what Mira thought, it wasn't what it might look like. Keisha's every sob seemed to contradict this.

Most people were still asleep, their hard slumber fueled by the exhaustion of the day. As Janna and Mira walked past me, I didn't know whether to acknowledge them or to pretend to be asleep. They probably wouldn't have noticed me or Jimmy either way—Mira was crying now, too, and Janna was taking that burden onto herself.

I craned my neck again to see Sara and Keisha. Keisha was a wreck, and Sara didn't seem to know how to work the salvage. For a brief moment, Sara's eyes caught mine. I was amazed at the intensity of blame I felt toward her—for being the older one, for being the one who had more power, for being the one I assumed was the instigator. And also, I had to admit, for being the one who wasn't part of our group of friends.

The look she gave me wasn't beseeching—she didn't want me to pull Keisha away like Janna had done with Mira. And it wasn't apologetic. It was just matter-of-fact. We both knew what was going on, and that it had reached its inevitable breaking point. The only question was which way it would break.

"What should we do?" I asked Jimmy.

"What can we do?" he asked back. "No way to put the bus in reverse and make time go backward."

Flora came down the aisle, using the back of each seat as a handhold. When she got to our row, she nodded to us and tried to smile. Then she plunged on, told Sara it would probably be best if she moved to another seat, then sat down beside Keisha and told her it was okay, there was nothing wrong with crying it out. Sara hovered awkwardly over them, and I thought there was something in the way she didn't really want to leave, something that made me feel a little less anger. It was only after she walked farther back in the bus and sat in a seat where Keisha wouldn't see her that Sara herself began to cry.

"Look," Jimmy said. At first I thought he was going to say something about Sara. But then I turned and found he was resting his head against the window, staring out, pointing. I leaned in to see what he saw. There were bends and a rise in the highway ahead of us, so we could suddenly see the long rows of taillights wending their way west. There had to be hundreds of them, a long trail of red-bar Morse code, with only a few contrasting headlights moving the other way.

"Do you think they're all going to Kansas?" I asked.

"Yes," he said. Then he took my hand in his and closed his eyes again.

I knew how hard it would be to fall asleep while sitting on a bus, holding someone else's hand. I was too awake with thoughts, too awake with questions. With so many cars on the road in the middle of the night, with so many people crying in the close darkness of our bus, with so many uncertainties about what would happen to us, it seemed strange to think that this was our reality. But I guess that's what it was. And it was changing all the time.

fifteen

My parents and I never went on big vacations when I was younger. Mostly we stayed within a few hours of our house. Money was an issue—and then there was the matter of time, which was an even bigger issue for my family. Both my parents had jobs, and those jobs required them to work more and more hours as the economy worsened. Even when my mom was home with me, she was also at her workstation, trying to get her assignments done. I remember times when she would read her memos aloud to me in her best storybook voice, trying to trick me into believing that international travel restrictions were as transfixing as the location of wild things. Vacation days became voluntary for my parents, meaning that both of them were paid more if they left the office less. In a time when there were so many people out of work, replaced by computers and outsourcing, it wasn't like my parents were going to put up a fight. I was the only one who resisted. I wanted to go to Australia. I wanted to see the Grand Canyon. My parents had shown me YouTube videos, but it wasn't the same. I wanted to touch a koala. I wanted the Grand Canyon to hear my voice.

The older I got, the more I realized how lucky we were. In American history, most economic downturns were ended when young people were sent to fight wars. In this case, the President tried to start a war within our country to distract the people who were suffering on his watch. And even though we were Jewish and I was gay, I knew most strangers would look at my family and see white people first, and we'd get an advantage from that. It would be stupid to try to deny that.

Even when sickness spread and hate crimes against Jews and queer people increased, my family stayed safe. We tried to expand our bubble to include a regular life, but not expand it so much that it was thin enough to pop. If that was the price to pay for not traveling, I was willing to pay it.

Still, as the bus drove on through Ohio and Indiana and Illinois, I started to get a sense of everything I'd been missing. I was used to everything kinda looking the same— the same superstores, the same fast-food places, the same caffeine stops. I knew there were tens of thousands of each of them, spread out across the country, all dressed in the same architecture and, it felt, pumped with the same air. But what I hadn't counted on was the difference of the land. I thought I'd seen flatness before, but nothing at all compared to the way the highway stretched out across the plains, an infinitely straight line of pavement with exits that led to nowhere close. As we dipped a little south, the trees were still shedding their final colored leaves—green muting into shades of rust and coffee and mud. It all passed in a blur, but every now and then I would notice a detail—a hand-painted billboard urging salvation, two kids running through a field of grazing cows, a huge old statue of a brown-haired boy clutching a hamburger and smiling slyly. It made me sense the individuals in the multitude, the truth that not everywhere in America was just like everywhere else.

I wanted this to be encouraging rather than scary.

It was right before dawn on Sunday morning when we made it to Kansas City, Missouri, in the hopes of making a quick crossing into Kansas City, Kansas. But there weren't going to be any quick crossings that day—the sheer number of people trying to get into Kansas and farther on to Topeka was preventing that. By the time we got to the Kansas Turnpike it was a near-complete standstill.

"Kansas is turning into a parking lot!" Gus observed. "And this bus is starting to smell like a locker room."

This wasn't entirely true, but all of us were definitely ready for a shower and a change of clothes. We were used to seeing one another day by day, but we weren't used to being with one another day *into* day. Most of us were wearing deodorant, but it seemed to have taken the weekend off.

Gus wasn't going to let this mess up his style, though.

Somehow he managed to squeeze into the bus's coffin-size bathroom and change into a tight orange-and-purple T-shirt that read I'M TOO SEXY TO LET YOU STEAL THIS ELECTION.

On our news feeds, we saw the mass of cars and buses and trucks converging on Topeka—helicopters sent back pictures of highways that looked like strings of slowly moving beads. Some people gave up on their cars and started to walk—marching and chanting and plunging forward until they got to the state capitol.

"We won't take to foot yet," Virgil told us, "but I hope for your sakes that you wore comfortable shoes."

The governor of Kansas was still insisting on his recount, and all the old Decents were rallying around him. They said the future of the country was at stake—something we knew all too well.

For his part, Stein held multiple news conferences a day, encouraging more and more people to take part in the protest. For people who couldn't travel, Kansas Protests were being set up on the lawns of every state capitol in the nation. When I called my parents to check in, my mother didn't mention whether or not she'd go to the one in our state.

I was pretty sure Jimmy's parents were already at our capitol, setting up amps. When I told him this, he laughed.

"It's not so far from the truth," he told me. "They've set up a station to make banners."

We didn't talk about the conversation we'd had last night. It wasn't exactly like it hadn't happened—there was an added ounce of caution in our comfort, and there wasn't anywhere else it could have come from. But we seemed to have wordlessly agreed to let it go. I needed to believe he wasn't thinking about it, and he needed to believe I wouldn't make him talk about it anymore. We added it to the list of invisible truces that made up a living relationship.

"I bet my grandparents are locking their doors and barricading themselves inside," Jimmy went on. "They live in Tallahassee, only about ten minutes from the capitol building. They must be treating this like the eleventh plague."

I knew immediately which grandparents Jimmy was talking about. While his mother's side was a mix of almost every race and background imaginable, his father's parents hadn't been too happy to have their son marry someone who wasn't as Black as they were.

"They never got it," Jimmy told me now, shaking his head. "What my parents did—that's what all of America should be doing. Love who you want to love. Have children who are such a mix that it blurs everything. Make us all a mix, you know? You can't hate someone so much for being different when their blood contains some of yours. It's so simple. But my grandparents—they don't get that at all. They wouldn't get us at all."

It felt good to be part of an "us," even if it was being defined by the people who wouldn't understand.

I could only imagine what Jimmy's grandparents thought of Alice Martinez, Stein's vice president. I remembered sitting next to Jimmy on the day she accepted her nomination, watching awestruck from Jimmy's couch as she said:

*

"I am proud that I defy your categories. I am proud that I don't fit easily into any box. I am proud of all the things I am and all the things I can be. Question yourself every time you think you only see one thing in me. If you're seeing me only as a woman, think again. If you're seeing me only as Latina, think again. If you're seeing me only as Black, think again. If you're seeing me only as straight, think again. If you're seeing me only as a politician or a mother or a daughter or a sister or a citizen of my town, my state, my country, my world—think again. I am all these things at once, and I am going to put every last one of them to use."

I knew Keisha had also been moved by Martinez's words; she often told us that she was as much a Martinez supporter as she was a Steinhead. It was hard to see much of that spirit now, though. She, Mira, and Sara had stayed as far away as possible from one another since the dimensions of their triangle had been revealed.

The bus didn't seem big enough to contain all the tension. Even though it was cold out, we opened windows wherever we could. We wanted air—any air that hadn't been sitting with us for hours.

Finally, Clive needed to stop for fuel, so we were all released into a rest station a few miles short of Lawrence. Virgil told us to be back in twenty minutes and swore he'd leave without us if we straggled.

"Gonna make you *sweat*," he said, chuckling. Flora hit him in the arm.

This was our first waking break since the previous night, so when we walked out of the bus we were hit momentarily by the shock of daylight, air, freedom, and time. It didn't take me long to notice that the rest area had divided itself roughly into two factions—with Steinheads keeping to one part and the opposition keeping to another, with only the restrooms and the food counters witnessing a tense intermingling of the sides.

I lost track of everybody while I used one of the bathroom mirrors to aid me in reconstructing my hair into something that looked like a style and not a follicular homicide. Once I managed to product myself into presentability and razor through the rubble of my stubble, I emerged to find Gus surrounded by three guys whose hotness made my thermometer spike to feverish heights.

"Duncan!" he called out to me. "Come meet the triplets!"

It was soon explained that Glen, Gary, and Ross had hitchhiked from Greenfield, Ohio, to get to Topeka in time for the march. Glen and Gary were both gay; Ross was not. But they were identical in all sorts of other ways, including their dimples, their bright-sky eyes, and their willowy light blond hair.

"We have room aplenty for them, don't we, Dunc?" Gus asked.

"I'm sure we can find a way for them to squeeze in," I replied.

"Super awesome!" Gus cheered, then grabbed Glen's hand to lead the brothers back to the bus.

Gus wasn't the only one of us making new friends. Mandy had met an elderly woman named Mrs. Everett on the line for the loo. Mrs. Everett was a choir director from Chattanooga who'd come up with her church to march for Stein. When Mandy mentioned where they were from, Mrs. Everett said, "Why, you must know Virgil, then!" Mandy promised a reunion once their wait was over.

Jimmy met a guy named Elwood, who was from Tonganoxie, a town a few miles away. He said he'd escaped his parents to take his stand in Topeka. He was eighteen but still in high school, and determined to get there, no matter how many people forbade him from going. Watching him was like seeing a match starting to burn, and Jimmy promised him space on the bus if there was any left to be had. He told us he'd never been so far from home before.

On the other side of the rest stop there were people who clearly would've preferred to slash our tires. One woman wore a shirt that said THE OVAL OFFICE IS NO PLACE FOR A SODOMITE, while another guy wore a cap that said THIS IS MY COUNTRY . . . DON'T MESS WITH IT. One mother stopped her children from playing with a kid with a Stein sticker on his backpack, as if he were contaminated. It was so sad to me, that politics could get in the way of kids playing. But it wasn't a surprise. It felt like at some point, a whole lot of politicians had lost their desire to collaborate. Government is supposed to be collaborative by its nature, but the competition had drowned that out and spread into the cracks of families and friendships. It made me really afraid, because if *divide* was successful, then *conquer* couldn't be that far behind.

I walked over to where Janna and Mira were feasting on fries and taking a good look around. The two of them had been inseparable since last night's fallout moment, as if Mira had subbed in a friend to make up for the absence of a girlfriend.

"What's going on?" I asked, as innocently as possible.

"Did you have any idea? Was I that blind?" Mira wanted to know.

"Don't ask him that," Janna said. "I'm sure he was as surprised as everyone else."

"I can't believe it," I said, which wasn't exactly an untruth. "What're you going to do?"

"I don't know," Mira said. "I honestly have no idea. Just be hurt for a while, I guess. The anger passed pretty fast."

When I got back to the bus, I discovered that we'd found room not only for the triplets but also for Mrs. Everett, Elwood, and a boy our age named Sue, whose story I didn't know yet.

Gus pulled me aside and said, "Hombre, I'm totally triple-crushing on Glen!"

"How do you know he's the one you're crushing on?" I had to ask.

"Oh, it's so ultraclear," Gus confided. "With Ross, I'm groin-crushing. With Gary, it's groin-crushing and a little mind-crushing. But with Glen—whew!—it's groin-crushing, mind-crushing, and heart-crushing. The triple, you see? I'm feelin' all bursty! Is it more obvious than obvious?"

I assured him it wasn't, then told him his hair looked really good, which made him feel much better.

"Thanks, Dunc," he said. "Now I gotta go get me a window next to his aisle."

True to Virgil's word, we were back on the road twenty minutes after we'd arrived. Traffic was moving at the speed of syrup now, but at least it was still moving. We were skipping Lawrence and heading straight to Topeka, worried that any detour might mean missing the big event.

I was sitting a little more toward the front than I had been before, since Jimmy had asked Elwood to sit by him so they could talk. I could've gone back and sat with Keisha or Sara, but decided that would be too fraught. So instead I paired up with Mandy, who was checking their phone every two minutes for a new traffic report.

About ten minutes into the ride, a figure stepped into the front of the aisle, right by the driver. It was Mrs. Everett, and since we weren't moving very fast, it was easy for her to keep her old frame steady as we went.

In a voice forceful with conviction, she said to us all, "I would like to tell you how I came to be here."

A few conversations in the back shifted to murmuring, but for the most part we all fell silent.

"Thank you," Mrs. Everett continued. "My name is Ida

Mae Perkins Everett, and the Lord is the reason I am here today. I am an old woman, and I have to tell you, old women like me usually like to stay home. Every time I take a step, I can feel parts of my body that I'm sure none of you except my good friends Virgil and Flora ever notice. Like your hip. How many of you ever feel your hip?

"All's to say, this is not an easy journey for me to make. If I didn't think I was doing the Lord's work, I don't know that it would be enough to get me out of bed. I'm not saying the Lord Almighty has talked to me directly. I'm not saying He came down from the heavens and said, 'Ida Mae, I want you to get yourself to Kansas to help that Stein.' The Lord's got more important things to do than planning my schedule for the week. No, He ain't gonna tell you what to do. You just have to read the Lord inside of you. You gotta know what you know, and then you have to act on it. I voted for Stein because I believe in the things he believes. But I know from the Lord that believing isn't always enough. Sometimes you gotta take your body and put it on the line. Jesus could've just stayed at home, you know. He didn't have to do a blessed thing. But he headed out into the people. He wanted to inspire lives besides his own. He knew to work for something greater, and that's the greatest thing of all.

"So I came here with my church. And, lo and behold, who do I find at a rest stop but the man who taught me how to dance? I know you won't necessarily believe this, but it wasn't too long ago that Virgil and I were kids like yourselves. Hard to picture, I'm sure. I wish I could say we were as smart as we are now, but back then we still had many miles to go before we got to total sense. We thought the best thing in life was enjoying ourselves, and, Lord, we enjoyed ourselves! If you needed a dance floor cleaned, you didn't need to pick up no mop. All you had to do was invite Virgil to the party and he would shine it all with his body, breakin' and groovin' and getting all the rest of us to sweat it out. He'd make me dance 'til I didn't have any dance left, I tell you, and even then I'd keep going 'til the sun came up. It was fun—and I'm not one to knock fun. But there was one thing missing, and that was the everything else. The greater. We were so into ourselves that we didn't realize the changes that were happening around us. We were—if you pardon the phrase—screwed over and screwed over and screwed over without recognizing who was screwing us. Finally, though, we saw the light, and we realized that fun is fun, but you also need to pay your dues. And I don't mean to the guy at the door.

"I'm an old woman, and I'm still paying those dues. Still trying to have fun, too, which is why I ditched on my lady friends to be here with you. Not just because of Virgil, although he's as foxy as ever. It's easy to think that everything's gone to H-E-L-L when you get to be as old as I am. But let me tell you—the 'good old days' were much worse for a lot of us. People aren't the only things that get better with age."

She turned to look at Elwood, who was almost vibrating with excitement.

"You," she said. "How old are you?"

"Just eighteen," he answered, trying to sound tough, like a puppy barking loud.

"And what's your story?"

Elwood stepped into the aisle, facing Mrs. Everett. The silver studs in his black jacket shone in the daylight coming through the windows, crowned by his silver belt buckle, which he definitely needed in order to keep his pants on his line-straight body.

"I'm from Tonganoxie," he began, his soft-spoken voice returning. "I doubt any of you have ever heard of it or been there. No reason to, really. I'm here because my parents suck. I mean, they massively suck. When the history of suckdom is written, their faces are going to be on the cover. Suck is their home page."

"And why do they suck?" Mrs. Everett asked, looking amused.

"They suck because they won't let me be myself. They won't let me be . . . Jewish!"

"What, child?"

That was all Mrs. Everett needed to ask. Suddenly the words came pouring out of Elwood.

"They won't let me be Jewish! They say it's just a phase, but it's not a phase—it's something I've always wanted. And even though they're not religious they say that I can't be Jewish because they're not Jewish and they think Stein is the only reason I want to be Jewish, but I wanted to be Jewish ever since I was seven and I was watching Saturday services online and it just seemed so holy, and I thought if Jesus was a Jew why can't I be a Jew because I love the prayers and the Hebrew and the way they've triumphed over all this massive hate for so many centuries, and I don't know if I can be strong like that, but if the oil in the lamp in the temple—you know, during Hanukkah—if that lasted for eight days—just one drop—then clearly miracles happen and me being Jewish isn't anything close to being a miracle, it's just something I want to do. I was perfectly happy keeping it a secret and learning Hebrew online and seeing the services and giving myself a Hebrew name, but the thing is that even though I'm long past thirteen I really want to become a bar mitzvah. There's no synagogue anywhere near me, so I figured the time had come to tell my parents, and even though I knew they sucked, I had no idea that they ultra, ultra sucked, because they wouldn't even hear what I was saying when I told them I had emailed with the rabbi at a shul in Kansas City, and he was willing to help me prepare. I told them I would pay for it with my own money. I told them, yes, I'd met other Jews online, but, no, they didn't convert me, this was something I wanted to do all on my own. Plus, Jews don't do the whole missionary thing. But my parents—well, they went through the roof in about sixteen different places and said that while they put up with the way I dress and the music I listen to, they could not put up with me being Jewish and having a bar mitzvah, and I told them it's *becoming a bar mitzvah,* not *having a bar mitzvah,* and that was the last thing they wanted, me correcting them on how to say things, so they got ultra mad and I realized part of what Stein has to put up with every day, and I realized if no one was going to support me, the least I could do was go and support someone else—a fellow Jew, who maybe as President can make all the people who suck have less power. So I left. I mean, even though it was Sunday I pretended I was going to school, and my parents suck so much they didn't even notice. I hiked my way to the rest area and that's where I met Jimmy, and he says it's cool for me to be Jewish, and I think that's just the nicest thing anyone's ever said to me. I hope he's right because I'm going to do it one way or the other because that's who I am and that's what I want and I don't see what the big deal is, either. Which is, I guess, why I'm here."

Quickly, he sat back down in his seat, with Jimmy giving him a big thumbs-up sign. Mandy and I started to applaud, and soon everyone was doing it, Mrs. Everett loudest of all. Elwood blushed a traffic-light red and wouldn't meet anyone's eyes for the next few minutes.

When the applause had died down, Mrs. Everett looked at the triplets and asked, "How about you?"

Ross stood first.

"I'm here for my brothers."

He sat down and Gary stood up.

"I want to be where the action is."

Then Gary sat down and Glen stood up, sending a look loaded with sweetness Gus's way.

"I'm going to Topeka because I want to make sure nobody steals this election from under my nose," he said. "And I'm here on this bus because I was totally hitting on Gus at the rest area, and he was totally hitting on me. I knew right away that he was rainbow sprinkles, and he hasn't proven me wrong yet."

Gus beamed like a thousand stars piled in a bus seat. The rest of us tried not to be skeptical.

Finally, Mrs. Everett looked at the boy named Sue and asked him what his story was. His hair fell in his eyes as he talked.

"Well, my daddy left my ma right after I was born," he began. "But before he did, he named me Sue. My ma loved him, so she said, 'All right.' It sure was hard on me at first. The other kids would make fun, and the guys Ma brought home would laugh and laugh and say I needed to get a new name. Oh, I hated it for sure. But I had a secret, too: Deep down, it felt right. Deep down, I felt like a Sue. I don't know how to describe it. There are some things you just know, and one of them is whether your name is right or not. Everybody else thought I had the wrong name. They said my daddy was a drunk and this was his last big joke. But I started to think maybe he had an ounce of the sight to him, even if he had a strange way of showing it. I just needed to find out— did he know something or was he kidding? I vowed I'd track him down and ask him.

"As soon as I got my license, I started to drive around. Then one night I drove into Gatlinburg and headed for the nearest bar. Something was calling me there—I can't really explain it. Sure enough, I spotted a man at the bar who just looked like the picture of my daddy that my ma kept hidden in her bottom drawer. Only now my daddy was dressed like my ma and had tits to spare.

"I walked right on up to him and said, 'My name is Sue. How do you do? You may be a woman, but I know you're my daddy.'

"Now, that remark hit her hard. But she recovered quick, pushed me straight out of the bar and into the street. I couldn't tell whether she was crying or whether it was just drinkin' tears I was seeing. I started yelling at her, going, 'Why did you name me Sue? Why? WHY?' And she was laughing and crying and cursing and then smiling. 'I'm Sue!' I screamed. 'I'm Sue!' And finally she just looked at me and said, 'I know you are, honey. I know.'"

Sue took a deep breath, then continued. "She said she knew this wasn't an easy world, and thought, maybe right, maybe wrong, that having her around would make it harder. She said she named me Sue because she wanted me to know all the things I could be inside. That when I was born she looked in my eyes and saw the deepest kind of reflection, which made her feel that everything she'd done wrong could be done right by me. She said, 'I gave you that name to leave you open to anything. Plus, I figured if you didn't like it, you could always change it. I'm guessing you must've kept it for a reason.'

"I'd never told anyone why I'd kept it, but now with this woman who was my daddy standing in front of me, I could finally admit that the name felt right. That even though I was a boy—still am—there were parts of me that liked being a girl. I didn't want to be a full girl or anything, like some of my friends or like my daddy. But I wanted to be a boy named Sue. There are lots of us out there—we know the names we're called don't really matter unless we feel that they're right. And I guess that's why I knew I had to help Stein and Martinez. Because they're boys called Sue, too. And I know my daddy would be proud of me for standing up for them."

"We're proud of you, too, son," Virgil said. "And that's the truth."

At this point, I couldn't believe that I'd hesitated in considering whether or not to come. I realized how easy I had it, and how lucky I was. And what good was luck if you couldn't pay it forward in some way? What good was good if you couldn't make it last longer and spread it wide?

I needed words to fuel me. I didn't need to be told what to do; I just needed to know that what I was doing had some worth. The words could be as simple as *thank you* or *you're welcome,* or as complicated as a story or a speech. The words could come from Jimmy, or Janna, or Stein, or these random people who'd arrived on our bus.

It was enough to let me know that the words in my head weren't alone.

They had a world in which to fit.

They would be heard and understood.

It felt like a lot to ask, in a world where people were so

busy broadcasting themselves that there was hardly enough time or inclination to listen. But why not ask a lot? Why not demand that people step away from presenting themselves to the world in order to understand the world as it was and as it needed to be?

I wasn't sure it was possible to focus on something so big. I'd never tried. Maybe because I felt safe, and when you're safe, you don't want to think too much about the things that are keeping you safe. It was possible that Elwood and Sue had understood the threat before I had.

The thing about having your eyes open is that you always have the option of closing them again.

I resisted the urge of safety. I tried to keep my eyes looking forward to the election we had to save, however we could.

sixteen

A few hours later, Stein addressed us.

"We will demonstrate peacefully and positively. We will show our opponents the power of peace, and send the world a message that we are a country that loves peace above all else. Our presence—millions upon millions of us—will be enough. We will raise our voices, but not our fists. We will show strength through solidarity, not aggression. Like the saints, we will go marching in . . . and we will march, and we will march, and we will march until justice prevails."

I kept rolling the phrase *power of peace* over in my mind. It felt like our whole society had been designed to make us believe the opposite—violence was power, physical strength was power, victory on the battlefield was power.

At the same time, I thought: If there are so many forces trying to work against peace, then when it actually happens, it must be *really* powerful, to withstand all that's aiming to tear it apart.

I wish I could say that everyone on this bus was talking about these things, about how to defend justice and empower peace. But it's hard to live on that level. Instead, some people were napping. Others were texting. And still others were dealing with the human drama unfolding in our midst.

Jimmy was sitting now with Mira. It was like the whole geometry of the bus had shifted to allow Mira as much room as possible away from Keisha or Sara.

"I don't know if I can ever trust her again," Mira told Jimmy. I sat behind them, with Elwood napping on my shoulder. "What she did takes everything away."

"You can't just erase everything," Jimmy replied.

"That's easy for you to say. You have Duncan. You're lucky."

"I know," Jimmy said. "I know."

From the front of the bus, Mrs. Everett and Virgil started singing a song about how everything is everything, how what is meant to be will be.

"Change," they sang, "it comes eventually."

*

Clive drove the bus as far as he could take it—but eventually all the traffic became a standstill, and we knew we'd have to walk the rest of the way. We'd crossed through the ring of chainmarts that surrounded Topeka, all the familiar names from Anywhere USA greeting us with their usual indifference. Cars and buses filled all the parking lots, but nobody was shopping. They were all heading to the center of town.

Our bus was parked in front of a sports store. We gathered the bare-minimum supplies, planning on a few hours' stay. Virgil took the lead, with Flora and Mrs. Everett beside him. Sara said she'd take up the rear. It was strange to see her and Virgil split like that—we were so used to them working in tandem. I couldn't tell whether the Keisha thing had thrown off that tandem or whether they were simply applying the basic kindergarten-field-trip rule of having someone in front and someone in back to keep the kids from getting lost.

There was a good chance of getting lost, because thousands of people were streaming past us now, each street a tributary uniting at the center of Topeka. There were individuals and couples walking, for sure. But mostly there were groups. Church groups and youth groups and work groups. Groups of friends, groups of family, groups of volunteers. Although it was clear (from signs carried, from comments overheard) that some of the people had come to protest our protest, most were Stein/Martinez supporters experiencing the power of arrival. No matter how far they'd traveled or what they'd had to leave behind, they were—like us—galvanized by the enormity and the intensity of our mission. It was as if the rally was a large and powerful magnet; the closer we got, the stronger the pull.

Sara's friend Joe and some of the other college-age volunteers split off into their own camp. Although nothing had been said, I felt that Jimmy and I had inherited Elwood as our buddy, because he needed some support as he ventured out into the world for the first time. His parents were not happy when he called to tell them where he was. My own parents were less angry but similarly nervous when I called with my own updates. The first time, I'd expected my father to be miffed at me for defying the law that he and my mother had laid down. But she must have gotten to him somehow, because all I received was an order to stay safe and to come back home as soon as it was over.

None of us needed a map of Topeka to know where we were headed. We just followed the flow, merging in with the other groups. We didn't mingle—most groups kept to themselves at this point, concentrating on sticking together rather than making new friends. Gus and Glen were a major exception to this rule. In just a few hours, they'd become unquestionably inseparable. If Gus's hand wasn't on Glen's shoulder, Glen's hand was on Gus's waist. Or their sides were so close together that it looked like a three-legged race. Gary and Ross, walking four steps behind, seemed amused. I still couldn't tell them apart.

"Did they really just meet?" Elwood asked Jimmy and me.

"Yup," Jimmy said.

"Wow," Elwood replied, admiring. But his eyes didn't grow wide until a few minutes later, when Jimmy told him that I was Jewish.

"That's ultra cool," Elwood said with an awed gasp.

Soon he was barraging me with questions about Torah reading and Yom Kippur and becoming a bar mitzvah and the story of Jacob wrestling with the angel. I answered him as best I could—about reading without vowels and repenting by throwing bread into a river and chanting something you don't completely understand (and also still not knowing what Jacob's ladder really means). None of these things had ever struck me as out of the ordinary, but explaining them to someone who found them extraordinary made me suddenly see a little more of their meaning. It also made me realize that a lot of the time when people talked about being Jewish, it was in the context of other people hating us. I was proud of all the times we'd survived attempts to annihilate us . . . but those events loomed so large that I didn't get to be proud of the things from the happier times. I had to define my Jewishness in part by the very real threats against us.

While Elwood had struggled against being prevented from being a Jew, I'd been conscious of the things that I thought being a Jew might prevent me from becoming. Really, there weren't that many—there had already been plenty of Jewish movie stars and senators and sports heroes and world leaders. The only office we didn't seem able to attain was the Presidency . . . until Stein.

I wasn't completely naive—I knew there were still plenty of people out there who'd like to keep us out of their private clubs. But still—once you knew there were enough people out there to vote for a Jew for President, you couldn't help but feel that anything else was possible. It had been the same with the first Catholic President and the first Black President. And it was definitely the same with the first gay President, who happened to also be the first Jewish President . . . as long as we could make his election in Kansas stick.

And even then, I knew: The people who hated us would probably hate us even more. Stein would be their reason, their cover, for blanket attacks. Just like the election of the first Black President hadn't erased racism, Stein's election wouldn't erase antisemitism or homophobia. It would inflame it . . . but that was no reason to leave the ceiling intact. You have to rise in order to rise above. You build something strong enough to withstand the backlash.

The closer we got to the center of the city, the closer the people were packed together. Some groups started cheers and chants—

"One-two-three-four / We won't take this anymore / Five-six-seven-eight / Good will triumph over hate."

"People say all over town / No way to keep a Stein vote down!"

"What do we want? / FAIRNESS! / Where we gonna get it? / KANSAS!"

—while other groups sang hymns and protest songs. As we all pressed together and heard the copters overhead, I could also hear Janna and Mandy whisper-singing behind me, a private golden thread of "Amazing Grace" sung not out of protest but out of faith. They had said their Sunday morning prayers earlier, and now their voices harmonized effortlessly, since it was a song they'd summoned so many times before to underscore their beliefs. It was amazing, and it was graceful, and it was that most rare of things—a sound that makes us see.

When they were through, we turned on the news and heard that the number of people alongside us was definitely over half a million, possibly over a million, with more and more arriving every minute.

After about an hour's worth of walking, we reached downtown. The flatness of the land was mirrored in a flatness of architecture. The walls were bland or blank or brick, the windows empty or blinded. It felt like the kind of place that always seemed shut down. The locals looked shell-shocked for the most part, unprepared for this sudden invasion of easterners and westerners, northerners and southerners. A few, however, had decided to profit from the occasion and were selling bottles of water for ten dollars each. At this point, they had very few takers.

We fell in step with a church group as we reached the street leading to the rally. The police had divided the street roughly in half, with the Stein rallygoers veering to the left and the Decent protesters roped off to the right. The opposition candidate had decided to have his own rally in Wichita at the same time as Stein's in Topeka, but there were still thousands of anti-Stein people here, yelling and jeering at us as we passed.

"Don't pay them any attention," Virgil warned.

Still, it was hard to ignore them. No matter how loud we chanted, their dissonance was thrown at us. So I looked, and Jimmy looked, and what we saw nearly stopped us cold. There were only a few signs with Stein's opponent's name on it—these people weren't pro-him as much as anti-us. So instead of mass-produced campaign posters, there were hundreds of handwritten signs.

STEIN IS A SODEMITE.

THE MEAK SHALL NOT INHERIT THE U.S.A.

GOD SAYS FAGS SHOULD DIE!

GO HOME JEW FAGS—THIS COUNTRY ISN'T 4 U.

I recoiled, tried to back away from them. But Jimmy took my hand and held it tight. Held it so everyone could see it. Held it to defy them.

We got their attention. Suddenly the yelling was directed at us. Telling us to go home. Telling us to die. Telling us we had no right to be here.

I could feel myself going defensively blank, shutting down. Which is exactly what hate wants to happen—a complete diminishment in the face of its fervor. People think these hateful things, and you know they do, and it saps you of energy you might otherwise be using to live your life. When they say them out loud, when they throw these words in your face, it's meant to startle you into submission, shake you away from your foundation so they can knock your walls down.

I could sense Jimmy getting angrier and angrier. The pastor from the church group next to us tried to block us from the taunts, his face full of concern. One of the Decents decided to throw something at us—just a plastic juice bottle, not something that could really hurt. It hit the pastor instead, the leftover juice spraying the three of us.

That was it, as far as Jimmy was concerned. He was about to charge them, about to curse and yell and fight if he had to. And I—well, I held his hand tighter. Even as he started to pull away, I held on, dug in. He was surprised, but he didn't let go. I pulled him forward a little. He resisted. Then the pastor looked at us and said, "Let's keep walking. Just keep walking." Brushing the juice off his jacket, asking if we were okay.

I wondered if anyone else had noticed. Then I got my answer: Janna and Mandy started singing "Amazing Grace" again—and this time it was loud, meant to be heard. The golden thread turned into a banner. The pastor joined in, and people all around us started to sing along. The Decents yelled louder, but they couldn't break the harmony.

'Twas grace that taught my heart to fear,
And grace my fears relieved.
How precious did that grace appear
The hour I first believed.

The pastor could tell I was still shaken and Jimmy was still enraged. Even Elwood looked ready to go back and make some trouble.

"Don't let them get to you," the pastor told us. "All they have is hate, and in the end hate is worthless. They want for us to become hateful, too, and to forfeit His love in our anger. When faced with such hate, we can only embrace love tighter. As Paul said, 'Love does not delight in evil but rejoices with the truth. It always protects, always trusts, always hopes, always perseveres. Love never fails.'"

I had not let go of Jimmy's hand. But now I tried to let my grip ease, to get us back to boyfriends instead of two boys under attack. We passed the last (for now) of the shouting Decents and made our way into the area in front of the Kansas statehouse.

Hearing that there were over half a million people present hadn't prepared me at all for the sight of it—the enormity of it. There were people as far as my eye could see, and I was sure there were people beyond that as well. Bodies and banners and signs, clothes of all colors, faces of all ages. Children on their parents' shoulders, people in wheelchairs. Muscle-shirted and journal-scribbling, picnic families and motorcycle gangsters. Holy Ghostwriter fans with bad haircuts and I'M 4 STEIN 2 B PREZ buttons. Proud Kansas voters for Stein, identifiable by their PROUD KANSAS VOTERS FOR STEIN T-shirts, with *Don't mess with my vote* written on the back. I couldn't stop taking it all in.

There were still about two hours to go before Stein would

speak, so there was no focus to the crowd, no direction that we all faced. From above we'd look like a gigantic mass, but under a microscope we'd be divided into our own cells, talking and eager with anticipation.

Once again, it felt like history. But this time our piece was even bigger.

Our group had managed for the most part to stay together. Virgil, Flora, and Mrs. Everett were fueling themselves on stories from the past, stopping every now and then to compare aches and pains. Sue kept largely to himself, searching the crowd around us from his singular place within it, considering each face before moving on to the next. A few feet away, Gus had planted himself and Glen on an old sheet he'd brought, and was regaling him with tales of his own misadventures.

". . . and then—no lie whatsoever—I found myself on the shore, drip-dry nude, and I thought to myself, *Only a fool like myself would break up with a vengemeister before going skinny-dipping.* I never got the clothes back, and had to borrow this cape from a noodle of a seven-year-old in order to make my way home. You wouldn't believe the major-wrong tan line I got that day. I can be such a void when it comes to boy issues."

"Aw, don't be so self-deprecating," Glen said, clearly charmed instead of alarmed.

"If I don't deprecate myself, who will?" Gus asked playfully.

"How 'bout I appricate you instead?" Glen offered.

"I'm ultra open to apprication."

A kiss immediately followed.

A long kiss.

An epically long kiss.

"They're going to need some oxygen when that's over," Mira observed from the side.

But neither Mira nor Jimmy nor I could really criticize—we'd all been like that, even if we might not have been quite so public about it. I had one of those momentary fantasies—one of those imagination side trips that last a little longer than a hope but a little shorter than a daydream—that Jimmy would lean into me now, whisper something snide and sexy like, *Hey, darlin', how 'bout you and I appricate each other, too?* and lead me into the same kind of kiss.

But Jimmy didn't seem to be paying too close attention to what was happening with Gus. I felt, in fact, that his attention was still back on the gauntlet we'd walked, stuck in the jeers and provocations that had been hurled at us.

"What's wrong?" I asked.

"Just moody, I guess. I know it's not really in accord with God's love, but I seriously wanted to go nuclear back there. I know it's a free country, but nobody should say those things. For whatever reason. Somebody needs to tell them that."

"Do you really think they'd listen?"

"No. But it would make me feel better, I guess. To know I didn't just let them get away with it."

"They only get away with it if we let it get to us."

"Not really, Dunc. I mean, think about their kids.

They're going to teach them to be just like them. How do you stop that?"

"By getting the world around the kids in better shape, I guess," I said. "I mean, if everyone was just like their parents, your dad would be just like your grandparents, and you'd be just like them, too. Which, I'm happy to report, isn't the case. I would have a really, really hard time making out with your grandparents."

Jimmy smiled slyly. "I'm sure they'll be relieved to hear that." Then he sighed. "It's bad enough that they're saying those things, and that politicians are encouraging them to say those things. They make us the enemy so they can keep those people's votes, even if they're always stealing money from them to give to rich people. That makes me even madder, you know? Hating us is just part of the game. But it comes at a real cost. And the politicians who stoke the flames, they don't care about the cost. They don't care about dead queer kids or hurt queer kids at all. Maybe that's what I'd like to tell those people with the signs. I don't think it would make a difference in the moment, but maybe later on, they'd realize we're not the enemy. We belong to God just as much as they do."

I nodded, unsure of what else there was to say. It felt like a trap had been set—we couldn't not talk about it, but the more we talked about it, the more we were letting them define our day.

Next to us, Mira said, "Hey, take a look at this!" and showed us the latest news on their phone.

*

Olivia Butler is the fourth Kansas election official to re-sign in protest of the governor's recount, and the ninth person directly involved in the elections to allege tampering on the governor's part.

"What's happening is politics, plain and simple. The governor promised his party the state, and he's doing everything he can to deliver it."

The governor's spokesman has labeled Butler as a Stein supporter whose own motives are political.

"That's just not true," Butler says. "I actually voted for the governor in the last election. But never again. What he's doing is wrong."

"Isn't this enough?" Mira asked. "I mean, how can anyone believe him now?"

Jimmy laughed. "It'll take much more than that," he said. "Why let a few inconvenient truths get in the way of your lie?"

"It doesn't matter what you or I believe," Virgil said. "It's about what they can get away with. That, I'm afraid, is the ultimate measure of a person: how they act when they're wrong but know they can get away with it anyway. Now, I have no doubt that the governor and everyone else on his side think they're doing the right thing. I'm sure they've managed to justify it in their minds. But the more people know they're wrong, the harder it will be to ignore it. The question is: When it's perfectly clear that they're up to no good, what will they do?"

"But Governor Nicols isn't a total pawn, is he?" Mira asked. "I mean, he actually has a pretty good record in pushing for universal health care in Kansas, and he spoke out against insurrectionists when he campaigned last year."

"You're right," Virgil said. "There's some good in his record. But right now, he has to be under enormous pressure from his party. So often it comes down to whether a politician can put the principle of politics over their own personal ambitions. That's the central dilemma of all political life. Some rise to it better than others."

There was a cheer from the front of the crowd, like an echo before the noise, which caused those of us farther away to pay attention. Thinking we were in the back of the rally, I turned around and found that, no, we weren't in the back at all—more and more people had arrived, and now the crowd was spilling out in every direction behind us. Speakers and screens had been set up all around town, and most of us had our phones out, too, to see what was going on up front. The speeches had begun, with politicians and movie stars and musicians and authors coming up for their minute of spotlight to say that Stein was and would be the next President of the United States. We were here, they vowed, to make sure of it.

Being in such a large group of people, I had a weird

flashback to the pandemic, that lost year or so when there wasn't any way to be united like this. And watching, after George Floyd was murdered, as people risked their health to be united anyway. Because being united mattered more. Because change needed to happen.

After the ninth or tenth speech, the cheering became a little more distracted. Maybe we were too busy taking in the situation to fully be a part of it. While Mira talked to Jimmy, Virgil, Elwood, and Sue, I noticed that Keisha and Sara had strayed from our group. I looked around and finally found them having a heated conversation about a hundred feet away from us, just in front of a group of dog lovers holding leashes and PUGS FOR STEIN banners. Both Keisha and Sara were crying and, from what I could tell, Sara was trying to argue Keisha out of what she was saying. It was unclear whether or not her arguments were working. But what was clear—shockingly clear—was that whatever they'd done wasn't just a stupid fling. Sara really cared about Keisha, to the point of pain.

Sara tried to come forward, to wrap Keisha back up in her arms, to embrace the conversation into being over. But Keisha shook her head, pulled back, said something else that made Sara step away and reply with something that clearly wasn't as pleading as before. Keisha rallied, pointing, telling Sara to go. And Sara did. She said one last thing to Keisha, then picked up her bag and pushed into the crowd, disappearing in a matter of seconds. Keisha just stood there, looking like a buoy in an empty lake.

Nobody else from our group had noticed. They were too busy paying attention to one another or to the speeches. I could have gone to Flora or Janna or Mandy, told them what had happened and asked them to check in with Keisha. But for some reason I felt I needed to go there myself, to finally talk to her, to see what I could do to make things better—or, if not better, at least bearable.

It was funny—I'd never really thought of myself as Keisha's friend or as Mira's friend. I'd thought of myself as Keisha-and-Mira's friend, because I'd always thought of them together. Now that they weren't, I hardly knew where I was.

When I got over to Keisha and said hey, she took one look at me and actually laughed.

"Damn," she said, "I thought *I* was the one who was supposed to be miserable."

She only found it funny for about three seconds, though. Then she was back inside herself, and I was somewhere else.

"How's it going?" I asked.

"I'd say it's pretty gone."

"Wanna talk about it?"

"I have a lot of wants right now. That might be in there somewhere. You're brave for coming to talk to me, you know."

"Why?"

"Because I'm the bad guy. There always has to be a bad guy."

I didn't know what to say to that. It wasn't exactly wrong. But it didn't feel exactly right, either.

She continued through my silence.

"I'll give you some advice, Dunc. Whatever you do, try not to fall in love with two people at the same time. While it's happening, you're haunted by knowing it's never gonna work out. And then it doesn't work out."

I tried to imagine being in love with someone else at the same time as being in love with Jimmy. But I couldn't, and told Keisha that.

"Believe me, I thought it was impossible, too," she said. "It wasn't like I was looking. I was more than happy with Mira. But then I met Sara and there was just this charge. I didn't choose for it to happen—it was there, and the only choice I had was to deny it or admit it. And I couldn't even manage denial. It would be like trying to say *I don't hear you* to someone screaming in your ear. I know it won't make sense to you, and I'm pretty sure it won't make sense to Mira, either, but it wasn't either/or—it wasn't like I had to fall out of love with Mira in order to fall for Sara. Yeah, those were supposed to be the rules—but feelings don't follow rules. Guilt does. Fear does. But attraction? No way."

"So you and Sara hooked up," I said.

"Not right away. But yeah. We couldn't stop it. Because we didn't want to."

I knew it was simplistic of me, but when I tried to put myself in the whole picture, I was sure that there was no way I'd ever be able to play Sara's or Keisha's role. No, I would always be Mira. As much as I hated to admit it—and would never have said it to him—while I was pretty comfortable in thinking that Jimmy would never cheat on me, I also knew that if one of us was ever going to do it, it was going to be him. So maybe that's why I found myself unable to tell Keisha I understood what she was saying.

"So you lied," I told her instead. It didn't sound judgmental at first, and it wasn't meant to be. I was just continuing the story she was telling. "You went off with Sara while Mira was oblivious. I have no idea if it's better or worse that you were in love with both of them—that'll probably hurt Mira even more. But whatever the case, you weren't honest. And then you go and make out with Sara in the back of our bus? You had to know you'd get caught. You had to know that Mira wouldn't stand for it. No matter how much you might still love her."

I didn't mean to make her cry, but whatever my intention, Keisha ended up falling apart again. The people with pugs—who were keeping a distance so carefully that you had to know they were listening to every word—didn't make any move to comfort her, so ironically that role was left to me, the person whose words had hurt her in the first place.

"Look," I said, "I'm sorry. I know you feel bad. I was just saying . . ."

Keisha rubbed her eyes, then waved the rest of my sentence away. "Don't," she said. "I didn't really expect you to understand. You and Jimmy aren't there yet. You're still honeymooning. Mira and I couldn't compete with that."

"What are you talking about? You guys were the model. That's one of the reasons this is so upsetting. I'm struggling all the time when it comes to me and Jimmy. But you and Mira—that was easy."

"You are *not* struggling with Jimmy."

"Are you kidding? I am *constantly* struggling. There are all these times when he's so great and I'm just . . . okay. I know he loves me and I know I love him, but for some reason I have to be the one who feels it more. I can be standing right beside him and still be missing him, because if he isn't entirely there with me I feel that emptiness. He doesn't, but I do. And now—well, now he's started to wonder how long it will last and I'm afraid I'm going to start to feel like I'm borrowing him, that eventually I'll have to give him back. I'll disappoint him too much and it'll be over."

I stopped there, feeling I should never have started. Why was I telling Keisha all this?

"The best you can do is try to make it work," Keisha said. "But that's no guarantee it'll work. If you and Jimmy don't talk about it, you should. Although right now I know I'm not the one who should be giving any advice."

As she said this, the crowd roared—Alice Martinez would be coming on in a matter of minutes, followed by Stein.

"It's going to be okay," I told Keisha.

"On one level, I know that," she said. "It's just not going to be okay in any way I once wanted it to be."

"Come on—let's get back to the group."

The true rally was about to begin.

seventeen

It was like a standing-only concert when the main act is about to appear—everybody pressing forward, closing up all the empty spaces. Keisha tried to tell me I was wrong about me and Jimmy, but most of her words got lost as we wound our way through the crowd in order to get back to our group. I managed to ask her where Sara had gone, and she told me she'd decided to spend the rest of the rally with her college friends.

When we got back, Jimmy shot me a look to ask where I'd been, then saw Keisha behind me and had his answer. Since Jimmy was standing close to Mira, Keisha peeled off and headed toward Gus and the triplets while I went back to where I'd been before. Other people pushed and prodded around us, trying to get nearer to the front, stepping over people's blankets and bags to get there. Something about all the movement and the closeness of it started to make me nervous. It was, I guess, another side effect of the reign of fear, when crowds were made to seem like dangerous things, vulnerable to the actions of a single person with a weapon and a willingness to use it. If isolation meant safety, then this was a high, high risk. We'd been taught to never trust strangers. *Fear thy neighbor* was what the deniers both practiced and preached.

I looked over to Elwood, who also seemed a little uneasy in the sudden press of bodies. I found myself rallying to lean over to him and say that everybody would settle soon enough.

"I've never been out of my county before," he said. "So this is . . . a lot."

I felt a body press against me from behind. Then the arms came wrapping around me again—the bracelet on one wrist, the watch on the other. I leaned back against Jimmy's chest, felt his breath against my ear, felt his unshaved chin gripple my neck. I tried to relax. I couldn't—not fully. But I tried.

"Ready?" he asked. Then, in a knowing whisper, he added, "Let's throw some tea overboard."

When I was a kid, I was obsessed with the Boston Tea Party. We didn't live near Boston, but that didn't matter. From the moment Mrs. Coolidge first mentioned it in my third-grade class, I was hooked.

•

We were talking about the causes of the American Revolution, and Mrs. Coolidge was listing them on the board.

Taxation Without Representation.

The Boston Tea Party.

The Coercive Acts.

The Boston Massacre.

. . . and so forth. I know the word *massacre* is the one that should have caused my eight-year-old mind to perk up, but it was the phrase *tea party* that truly lit up my thoughts. I imagined it as a sort of birthday party where tea was served, and wondered how it had led to a big war. Had someone important not been invited? Was the host not happy with their presents?

When I got home, I decided to act it out with my stuffed animals. The British officers were penguins, the American revolutionaries were dogs. They were all getting together to celebrate Betsy Ross's birthday, and she had decided to serve her special tea. (Betsy was played by Spotty, a beagle; I knew by then that I was a little too old to be referring to stuffed animals by their first names, but since I'd already given them their names when I was younger, I didn't see how I could suddenly stop using them now.) The party started with utmost civility, with everyone speaking in very clipped British accents. But then King George spilled some of his tea onto Thomas Jefferson. TJ leaped up, yelling that he'd been burned. Other British soldiers, thinking they had to follow their king, started pouring their cups of tea on the colonists.

Ben Franklin had tea poured in his eye, and Paul Revere's tail was dunked. Betsy Ross went off to cry in a corner—she hadn't even had a chance to open her presents!—while George Washington charged in and started throwing tea back on the British. Since they were penguins, they were particularly scalded by this attack—and suddenly the whole tide of the revolution had turned.

I thought I had the Boston Tea Party all figured out . . . for about an hour, until I went back to my room and did some searching on the internet. There, the real story unfolded—the unfair tax on tea, the ship parking itself in Boston Harbor, the colonists meeting to protest, then sending a group of men under cover of night to throw all the tea overboard. The details were fantastic—like how Samuel Adams and Paul Revere and the hundreds of other men darkened themselves with coal and *dressed themselves as Mohicans* before descending on the ship—because why would a bunch of white guys pass up a chance to throw the blame on someone else for their own misdeeds? What could be more American than that? A lot of the revolutionaries returned in their own boats the next morning to sink any of the tea that had been thrown overboard but hadn't been ruined yet. Nobody died, nobody was hurt. The British didn't even put up a fight. It was a great story.

For our class project that week, I made an elaborate diorama of the Tea Party, decorating an old model ship with angry colonists and placing it in a shoebox. I bordered the outside of the box with tea bags that had colonial slogans written on them, like *We're brewing some trouble!* and *We're Putting Your Tea on Ice!* and *We're having a party and taxes aren't invited!* Mrs. Coolidge was very impressed, and explained how the Boston Tea Party worked in no small part because the women and men in America were willing to give up something they truly loved—tea—in order to make the point that they couldn't be asked for money if they weren't going to have any say in how their colony was run. Personally, I couldn't understand what was so great about tea—I'd had some iced tea before, and unless you added a lot of sugar it tasted like sucking a tree. But I figured there weren't that many other drinks to choose from in 1773, so maybe tea was more attractive then.

For Halloween that year, I went as a member of the Boston Tea Party. Not dressed as a Mohican, but when anyone asked me about my costume, I brought up the inaccuracy and commented on the ridiculous wrongness of what Revere and the others had done. Instead of a candy bag I carried a big plastic ship. Whenever someone gave me a piece of candy, I dumped a tea bag from the ship and left it on their porch. I'd written *thank you* on each one.

I don't know exactly when my obsession with the Boston Tea Party ebbed back into an interest, and then a vague curiosity. Probably some other historical event came along and displaced it. Still, I kept the diorama on a shelf in my closet. I didn't even notice it there—it was as much a part of the room as the wallpaper or the stuffed animals that still perched on the top of my bookcase. One day early in our relationship, Jimmy came over and pulled it out, studying the sepia-toned tea bags and the colonists' dusty disguises.

"What's this?" he asked. So I told him about my obsession.

"I love it," he said when I was through. "The Boston Tea Party is so foundational. It's enterprising, it's righteous, and—most of all—it's excessive. I mean—you've seen paintings of Paul Revere, right? I'm sorry, but no amount of coalface was going to make him look like a Mohican. Or the rest of them. You have to ask yourself: What exactly were they thinking, dressing up like Mohicans and whooping their way down to the ships? I mean, do you think for a second that the British traders on the ships were fooled? If anything, they probably thought, *Whoa—these Massachusetts men are a little out of their minds, thinkin' they're native. I'd better stay out of their way.* And of course, now when people talk about the Tea Party, they don't seem to remember the way our Founding Fathers felt the need to pathologize and demonize and ultimately exterminate Indigenous people in order to get their freedom."

It made me think about it a little more. How I thought the Tea Party was a pretty good stunt, and I couldn't argue with the end result of independence . . . but like so many parts of our history, the bravery and courage of the revolutionaries were tarnished by their need to reaffirm their own superiority even as they gave lip service to freedom.

Jimmy and I both wondered aloud what the modern-day equivalent of the Boston Tea Party would be. Refuse to pay the fuel tax until we stopped having wars to get more fuel? Delete all social media apps from our phones so their revenue model would sink? Treat all bathrooms as unisex until gender restrictions on bathrooms were a thing of the past?

"I wish there was a thing called the Stupid Tax," Jimmy said, "which paid for all the stupid things our government does. We could just refuse to pay the Stupid Tax and let our money go to everything else."

"Yeah, but then what would we get to throw overboard?" I'd replied.

Now, standing in the middle of hundreds of thousands of people in Topeka, Kansas, I realized that maybe I'd put a little too much emphasis on the overboard part. I'd always thought the most revolutionary act of the Tea Party was hauling the crates of tea to the side of the ship and pushing them into the harbor. But really, the true revolution happened away from the docks. It happened in that first meeting place, where the colonists got together and realized something had to be done. And before that, when the people decided they could go without the thing they loved as a matter of principle.

Here I was, standing in the arms of someone I loved, having him whisper to me *Let's throw some tea overboard.* It was hard to imagine what Paul Revere would make of us— it was likely he'd get on his horse as fast as he could and ride in the opposite direction. But I liked to think he'd understand exactly what we were doing. This time we weren't going to wear a disguise to blame someone else. We were simply ourselves. Unmasked. Unarmed.

Ready.

"My fellow Americans," a prominent senator cheered, *"I present to you the next Vice President of the United States . . . Alice Martinez."*

eighteen

We all knew Alice Martinez's story—her rise from pov-
erty; her mixed heritage; her abusive ex-husband; her tenac-
ity as the mayor of Jacksonville and her tenure as a senator
from Florida. We were all familiar with Alice Martinez's
appearance—her straight black hair, always an inch north
of her shoulders; the color of her skin, the white of her smile;
the fierce intelligence of her eyes, which she refused to tone
down even when consultants told her she was coming across
as too smart, too unapproachable. But even if we'd heard
her story and seen her face hundreds of times, there was
still something electrifying about having her step onto the
stage to address us directly. From where we were standing,
I would have needed to zoom in two hundred percent to
distinguish her from any of the other people standing on
the stage. But still, it meant something to be sharing the
same space with her, no matter how big. It meant something

to share the same time and place, to know that even if she couldn't look into each of our eyes, there was an energy to us that she could use, just as there was an energy in her that made us stand strong.

She greeted us, then applauded us—the sound of her two hands clapping reverberated like a quick marching beat through the speakers strewn around us. Then she talked to us about the challenge of Kansas, and how the governor's accusations were falling apart like a paper lie in an ocean of truth.

"I'm telling you this—our opponents are trying to play this game as it's always been played—in the back rooms, in the darkness, while they try to make their power as absolute as possible, disregarding the will of the people. They spread lies and misinformation. They try to use time to their advantage. And mostly, by the power vested in them by their investments, they try to use money and intimidation against us.

"Well, I will not be intimidated. I have been through enough in this life to know that you can't just sit there and take it, no matter how scary it is to defend yourself. The cruelest weapon of the abuser is denial. Telling you that it's all in your mind. Telling you they know the truth and you don't. Telling you what happened didn't actually happen. You're making it up. You're wrong. You're not to be believed. They want you in the dark, because when you're in the dark, they have more power. They can get away with more. They're in control.

"Well, if they want to force the darkness, we are going to shine a light. You know how this works. Sometimes it feels like all you have is a single, small flashlight to fight back with. But that's where others come in. One flashlight can't take on such darkness. Two flashlights can't. But imagine thousands of flashlights shining on the same place. Imagine millions of flashlights. Because that is what we are. Here, and in every state capitol in this nation. From Juneau and Honolulu to Tallahassee and Atlanta, the warm, bright light of truth is streaming into Topeka, and there is no place for the makers of deceptions and untruths to hide. Our light will not falter, because it emanates from our conscience, and our sense of right, and our knowledge of what needs to be done. We will not waver, we will not dim, and we will not turn away until justice is restored and this attempt to thwart an election is defeated.

"I thank you for being here. And I thank you for standing strong. It is now my pleasure to introduce the popularly and electorally elected next President of the United States of America . . . Abraham Stein!"

How do you describe the sound of a million people cheering at once? It was as if the air became so saturated with our voices that we were breathing sound. If I'd taken every conversation I'd ever had, every cheer I'd ever raised, every song I'd ever heard, and played them all at once, it would have sounded something like the crescendo of goodwill now being released. As Stein walked onto the stage, we could not stop clapping, yelling, whooping. Gus put two fingers in his mouth and whistled loudly. Virgil's eyes grew teary. Janna and Mandy sang out. Sue hollered joyfully and Elwood ululated. Jimmy held me tighter and let me clap and cheer for both of us. It was something beyond a standing ovation. It was a *living* ovation.

"I thank you all for coming here and joining me to stand up for truth, justice, and democracy. I am told there are now over a million of you here in Topeka, with more arriving even as I speak. There are seven million more of you in front of the capitols of every state in this nation, and countless more watching this all over the United States and around the world. Your reaction has been swift, sincere, and strong. Your faith, like mine, remains resolute.

"Whenever democracy is threatened, all the beliefs and understandings behind it are also threatened. Whenever a truth is challenged, the value of all truths is challenged. Abraham Lincoln knew this. He knew that the Civil War tested whether our nation, or any nation so conceived and so dedicated, could long endure. And in the Gettysburg Address, he articulated the hope, the desire, the mission that brings us all here today: 'Government of the people, by the people, and for the people shall not perish from the earth.'

"Let me repeat that: 'Government of the people, by the people, and for the people shall not perish from the earth.' I stand here before you of the people, by the people, and for the people.

I stand here not only to protect the votes of each and every one of you who voted for me, but also to protect the country of each and every one of you who didn't. This election was decided beyond a doubt four days ago. Thus we must stand up against the people who want to create doubt, instill fear, and subvert our democratic process.

"We will not be tricked. We will not be silenced. And we will not be moved. I will stay here until the truth prevails. I ask you, too, to keep protesting until this election comes to its full and fair conclusion. We do not ask, as Lincoln did, for a 'new birth of freedom.' Instead, we ask for the preservation of the freedoms we have long held dear, and for the affirmation of a nation that offers its citizens fairness, kindness, and truth. Let us join together until this challenge has passed. And then let us stay together to celebrate the promised land of life, liberty, and equality."

Everyone started cheering again, even louder than before.

The chant started. Only part of the cheer at first, then—as more and more people caught on—becoming the cheer itself.

We will not be moved.

We will not be moved.

We will not be moved.

Stein, Martinez, and their families were all onstage now, saying the words along with us. The screens set up in the crowds showed other people across the country saying it, too. It was like the power of prayer, hearing everyone say the same words at the same time and giving them the weight of meaning.

We will not be moved.

I had no idea how long it would take. I had no idea how it would work. But I knew instantly that I would stay until the very end. I would stay until truth prevailed.

Jimmy's voice was right next to mine. I wanted to kiss him, so I did. To add to the thereness of the moment. To say we would not be moved.

nineteen

Eventually, the chanting stopped. Eventually, a group of folk and soul singers took the stage, starting with "This Land Is Your Land" and pulling us through a medley that emphasized the patriotism we all felt, the patriotism of freedom and real equality. After a few songs, particles of the crowd began to retreat back to their cars, homes, or hotel rooms. The rest of us started to think about settling in.

I don't think anybody in our group had thought about staying beyond the rally. We were unprepared for Stein's request; it no longer seemed practical to commute back and forth from where we'd been planning to stay in Lawrence.

The governor of Kansas, however, wasn't as surprised by Stein's move. No more than ten minutes after our chanting had stopped, he announced that the crowd had to disperse, since the permit to be on public land had expired when the rally ended.

Stein's response: *We're staying.*

The governor's response to that: *Don't make me send in the cops.*

To which Stein said: *Just be sure to arrest me first. We'll be sure there are lots and lots and lots of cameras around so the world can see it.*

The governor backed down, at least for now. We figured he was already feeling enough heat as election officials undermined his claims. Throwing Stein in jail would be the stupidest thing he could do.

So that obstacle was overcome.

Hundreds of toilet cubes were brought to the park—Stein must have rented every porta-potty in Kansas and Missouri. Rooms were procured for the sick and the elderly. Food distribution began.

And then there was the green.

During the rally, I'd seen them here or there—green flags and green banners, wordless and bright. As the sun dipped into the horizon, more of them started to appear, glowing in the dark. Vigilant in their vigil. Keeping watch over us all.

I didn't know who was handing them out until a kid came over to us with an armful, weighed down but proudly marching around, letting us take as many as we wanted for the night and possible days ahead.

As Virgil gathered us around, the sky still had some remnants of light in it, and the green material had yet to fully illuminate itself.

"A decision has to be made," he said. "You're all going to have to be honest with me, since we're in new territory here. None of you signed on to do this for as long as it takes—you were expecting to be home late tomorrow or, at the very latest, early the next day. Some of you have school. Others have jobs. We only have one bus, so we have to make this decision very carefully. We don't know how long this will go, or what's going to happen. For all we know, the governor might call in the National Guard to get us all out of here. Or some of the Decents, those fine people we saw with their hateful signs earlier, might take it in their own heads to make us leave. We have sleeping bags and some food in the bus, but we don't have showers or that many toilets or any of what you might call the creature comforts. We're not going to be partying like it's 1999—this is serious business. And if any one of you needs or wants to go, then we'll head back home and protest in Trenton instead. Now, what are people thinking?"

I couldn't imagine leaving. Not now, not from this. It would be like leaving the center of the universe. It would be abandoning a chance at being part of something big.

But I also remembered the promises I'd made to my parents. And I still had that fear that someone would come in shooting, or with a bomb. Just to show us who had real power in our country.

Nobody wanted to speak first—because nobody wanted to intimidate anyone who wanted to leave.

Finally, it was Elwood who said, "Well, we have to stay, don't we?"

Everyone else immediately chimed in. Virgil called Sara, who polled the other people from the bus.

"We have to stay," Jimmy murmured to me. I wondered if he sensed me wavering. Or maybe he just assumed I'd waver, because that was what I usually did.

Still, when the time came and I was asked, I said I wanted to stay.

In the end, it was unanimous: We were staying.

Calls were made to parents. Mine were not happy, to say the least. But they also realized there was no way to make me come back.

Jimmy's parents were thrilled. As we both knew they would be.

Suddenly, I realized what our decision meant: Tomorrow was Jimmy's birthday, and it was going to be spent here, in Topeka. I wondered if he thought I'd forgotten, since I hadn't mentioned it all day. I decided not to bring it up, and to think of some way to surprise him.

Virgil asked for volunteers to go back to the bus to retrieve supplies.

"Why don't you stay here with Elwood, and I'll get our stuff," I offered to Jimmy, thinking this would be the perfect opportunity to concoct a birthday plan.

Jimmy asked me if I was sure I didn't want him to come, but then Janna jumped in and said she'd go with me. Mandy made it sound like they really needed Jimmy to stay back and hang with them. So he said he'd stay.

Mira and Keisha both volunteered to go to the bus. Then, when they realized this, they both backed out.

"This is silly," Keisha said.

"Tell me about it," Mira mumbled.

It was the first time they'd talked to each other since "the incident." If you could really call it talking to each other.

"You go," Keisha offered.

"No, if you really want to, you do it," Mira said.

Finally Flora stepped in and determined that Mira would go and Keisha would stay. Then she said, "I want you two to think about working this out, you hear? Because it's going to feel like a long, long stay in Kansas if you're going to be like this. The quicker you work through it, the easier it's going to be for all of us."

Sadly, she didn't explain how they could actually "work through it." So they were left to their own poutings, which were almost humorously identical.

As soon as we were far enough away from our group's new base camp, Janna asked me what the plan was for Jimmy's birthday.

"I bought him a pony," I told her.

She slapped me on the shoulder. "That's so awkward— I bought him a pony, too!"

"Did you take the tag off? Can you still return it?"

"I bought it used."

"You bought my boyfriend a *used* pony?"

"Yes," Janna replied, looking skyward. "I bought him a pony that was used by the Lord."

"No! You don't mean—"

"That's right." She smiled. "Straight from the ark itself."

"Damn, that's one old pony."

"Only the most special for Jimmy."

I liked that Janna could joke about the Lord, even when she was such a firm believer. ("Although it doesn't really come up much in the Bible," she once told me, "I happen to think that Jesus had a great sense of humor. He just strikes me as the type.")

We talked some more about Jimmy's birthday. Then we got to the corner where the counterprotesters were. When I'd volunteered to go back to the bus, I hadn't been thinking about this part of the walk. Now I was swamped in dread. If anything, there were more of them now, shouting at us to go home, then telling us we were going to Hell.

"I wonder if Cathy's in there somewhere," Janna said as we passed. "I mean, if *Mary Catherine*'s in there. Cathy would never be a part of that. But Mary Catherine . . . I wonder if she's here, or if she and her family went to Wichita."

I scanned the crowd, looked at the faces. So many angry, tired faces. People just like us . . . but not like us, because they didn't like us. I didn't see Mary Catherine, but I saw a lot of Mary Catherines—girls and guys our age, shouting as loudly as the rest. Most of the counterprotesters were older, but there were still enough young ones for me to be painfully aware that this was a fight that would follow us into the future.

Janna shook her head. "I hope they don't think we're leaving. I want to tell them we're coming back. And that we're not going to Hell. I mean, who are they to say? It's one thing to warn someone out of concern. It's another to take it upon yourself to make the damnation. The last time I checked, it was the Lord's call whether or not we go down or up. I hope that whenever a person tells another person they're going to Hell that the Lord notices and decides to hold it against the Hell-caller when their day of judgment comes. I hope they get up to the gates and the Lord says, 'It was so easy for you to send people to Hell in My name that I'm afraid it's going to be easy for Me to do the same.' Who knows if that's how it works? All I know is that if you look at the Bible, you don't see Jesus telling people they're going to Hell. It just isn't right."

When we got to the farther reaches of town, we saw something inspiring: Although there were definitely some cars leaving now that the rally was over, there were still more people pouring into Topeka to join us. One pair of women passed us carrying a lime-green couch, preparing for the long haul. Their young daughter and son slept on top of it. It took us an hour to get to the bus, but along the way we were greeted by any number of smiles, nods, and determined looks. At the bus, Flora divided us into teams—some carrying sleeping bags and tents, others in charge of food and water.

Janna, Mira, and I were sent to carry some of the boxes of Everything Bars that we'd brought.

"A full day's nutrition in just one bar!" Janna chirped, mocking the Everything Bar jingle.

I tried to sort through the boxes to bring a balance of bars back to our base.

"Should I bring savory or sweet?" I asked.

"What do we have?" Mira asked back.

"A lot of Thanksgiving Dinner, some Cinnamon Goodness, some Fruit Attack."

"Ooh—I like Thanksgiving Dinner," Janna said. "Especially the blueberry dessert."

"I guess I'll just take some of each kind. Leave the rest for later."

"Do you think there's going to be a later?" Janna wondered aloud. "I mean, are we really going to be here for that long?"

I looked at the food supplies. "Well, it can't be too long. If we want supplies for the way back, we only have a day or two more for all of us, assuming the Everything Bars are enough to last the whole day."

"Are you saying they won't deliver as advertised?" Janna said, pretending to be shocked.

Flora came over to check on how we were doing.

"We got enough?" she asked.

"Absolutely," Janna said. "Even including the triplets and Sue and Elwood and Mrs. Everett."

"Oh, yes," Flora said. "*Mrs. Everett.* I tell you, that woman . . ."

Janna, Mira, and I were suddenly intrigued.

"How *do* you and Virgil know her?" Janna asked, making her voice as wide-eyed and innocent as possible.

"Hmpf," Flora said. "I guess you could say she was the one who came before me. Wanted Virgil bad, I tell you. But didn't catch him, and it's a good thing she didn't, 'cause I would've got him whether she had him or not, if you know what I mean."

I did know what she meant, and I was *scandalized*. I couldn't imagine Virgil with anyone besides Flora. They were like roots to the same tree.

"Are you worried now?" Janna asked. "I mean, now that she's back."

At this, Flora laughed and laughed and laughed—her whole body shaking like jelly in an earthquake.

"Whew!" she finally said, wiping the tears from her eyes. "That's a mighty good one. No, Janna, I'm not worried. Virgil liked her back when he was living la vida loca. That wasn't too long ago, but it's long enough. He's still got a streak in him, but it'd never really do him wrong."

"That's what I thought about Keisha," Mira said quietly.

"Oh, honey," Flora consoled, "it's not the same." She gave Mira a prop-up hug, then continued. "Virgil and I have some years on us now. And I'm going to let you in on a secret: When it all comes down to it, the thing that matters the most in a relationship is principles. Now, I'm not knocking the other stuff—even at our age, Virgil still makes my little red Corvette go much too fast. But what I'm really attracted to are his principles. We have the same idea of what's right and what's wrong, and that's gotten us through any number of things. If you can have that with someone, then you're most of the way toward love. Not just lover-love. Any kind of love." She smiled again. "If Virgil wants to dance with somebody who loves him, he's gonna be dancin' with me. Now let's get ourselves all packed up—the walk back's going to be much heavier than the walk here, so we'd better go while we still have some energy. Each of you might want to have one of those bars before we go."

I grabbed a box of Everything Bars and slung a sack of sleeping bags on my back. Janna packed some surprises for Jimmy in her pack, while Mira tried to avoid the inside of the bus altogether.

We stuck together more as we headed back: Mira, Flora, Clive, Janna, me, Gary, Ross, and the others in a delivery cluster. Flora mapped out another route that would take us a little longer but wouldn't subject us to the hateful hecklers. Besides the weight of what we were carrying, it was a pleasant walk—the weather hadn't turned to ice, and the stars were in evidence over us. The closer we got to Topeka, the more we saw the glowing green banners of the Stein supporters. What seemed like a whole squadron of schoolkids had spread out to distribute them, and everyone took them happily. We pinned the pieces of green to our packs and wore them across our shoulders. Just as we'd been a trail of headlights and taillights as we'd driven into town, we were now a hundred-lane highway of human traffic, all heading in the same direction, all looking for the same destination.

Every now and then, we checked the news to see if anything was happening. Nothing we saw or heard really surprised us—the governor of Kansas, unable to kick us out of his capital city, was now trying to play the fear card in a big way, warning everyone of disasters that could occur if we stayed, saying his troops couldn't be held responsible if they couldn't prevent "chaos among so many people who refuse to leave." He even mentioned the threat of tornados, even though tornado season was long over. Anything to get us to leave.

Meanwhile, more election officials were coming forward to say that Stein had won fair and square. But despite this, the governor's recount continued.

("They'll take it all the way to the Supreme Court," one commentator said. "And since the opposition party appointed the majority of the judges on the court, you can imagine what might happen there.")

Even though we'd changed our route, we couldn't avoid counterprotesters altogether. From a derelict-looking house, someone had hung a sheet that said WHITE LIVES MATTER. Out front, a disheveled man sat with a shotgun on his lap, looking like he couldn't figure out where his target was.

Flora seemed to add on to what Jimmy had said to me earlier. "It's sad. The opposition party is using these people just like they use everybody else. The politicians take those people's votes, saying they're going to bring back all that Decency. But then what do those politicians do? They take those votes and convert them into tax breaks for rich people. They don't even bother with following up on all that Decency talk. They promise anything to get the votes, then go back to ignoring the poor people until they need their votes again. Just goes to show: You can walk like a Person of God and talk like a Person of God, but that doesn't make you a Person of God unless you're willing to follow all the Lord's teachings."

"Hallelujah," Janna chimed.

"But what can we do?" Flora sighed. "No one likes to be told they've been duped. In a way, pointing it out makes it worse."

"Those poor people," Janna echoed.

"Don't think it isn't happening to you, too, dear. Your best interests are never the best interests of those who want to make money. They want you sick so you can pay for their cures. They want you anxious and feeling fat and ugly, so you can pay money to try to fix that, too. They want to fill jails so they can keep making money off of jails. They want to get rid of free public education so they can dictate what people learn and what people think is true. The real troubling part is, there isn't one mastermind behind it. It's just all these parts that fit together with the same goal. It's the road to ruin, but we're told it's the road to success. Jesus understood how wrong this is. That's why love was his currency, not gold."

We got closer to the park and saw what it had become. It was as if someone had taken the night sky and mapped it down onto the grass. Green specks glowed everywhere, blinking in the movement of bodies and breeze. The enormity of our gathering—so obvious in daylight—now took on the intimacy of a candlelight vigil, all of us united in an illuminated field. Already, children slept. Already, plans were being made for tomorrow. Voices traveled in long-distance conversations, and murmurs fell softly among couples and friends. We had all quieted into a settled hush. But that hush carried with it the potential of our noise . . . and the promise of what Flora would no doubt call our principles.

twenty

Everyone was happy to see us and the supplies. After we'd all eaten our fill, the sleeping bags were unrolled and the tents unfurled, each with a newly gained green-glowing flag at its height.

Since there weren't enough tents for everyone, Jimmy and I decided we'd sleep under the stars, zipping our bags together so we could be each other's furnace. Gus gave his own tent to Gary, Ross, and Elwood—and then he angled his way into getting our tent for him and Glen.

"I swear with all my heart and hips that I won't get him pregnant," Gus appealed to us (while Glen was out of earshot). "You know I'm saving it for my wedding night. But, oh my la, I'd marry him in a week and a day, if you know what I mean. It's like the first time we opened our mouths, our hearts just went leap-leap and have been snuggling ever since. That's got to be worth some tent space."

We gave him our tent and our blessing and some breath mints for the morning.

Mrs. Everett made a fuss about sleeping in the open air and seemed to want Virgil to invite her to stay close to him. Flora, however, swooped in and offered her son's tent . . . which she then set up herself, as far away from her own tent as possible.

Keisha came over to ask me quietly if I'd seen Sara by the bus or if I'd noticed whether Sara had taken her gear or not. I pointed out that there'd be no way for Sara to get into the bus without Clive's keys and said I hadn't seen her since she'd left. Keisha looked worried. "I'm sure she's okay," she insisted, "but I'd still like to know for sure." I told her to call Sara, and she said that she'd tried but hadn't received an answer.

Mira had gained custody of their tent, so Keisha was going to stay with Janna and Mandy. She tried to make it seem like this was okay, but I could tell she was sad about everything. Sad about Sara, sad about Mira.

I was glad that things were simpler with me and Jimmy. He was where I was supposed to be, and he was where I went. We zipped our sleeping bags together and nestled into each other as we grooved ourselves into the ground.

"Soon it will be your birthday," I whispered to him as we fell asleep.

"I hope I get my wish," he whispered back, then drifted away in my arms.

*

The tree Jimmy had planted for me for my last birthday was really a sapling. I'd noticed it immediately when I'd woken up and looked out my bedroom window that morning, and I'd known without a doubt that it had come from him. It was the best present I'd ever received. I could imagine it growing along with my life, along with our love.

At first, it needed a lot of care—Jimmy and I would take out the hose and water it gently, then spray each other and roll around until we were all grass stains and laughter. We watched as its first leaves turned the yellow of raincoats. Then we wrapped its base snugly when the chill set in. We knew that—like ourselves, like our love—it would eventually require less care, less attention. Someday it would be able to take care of itself. It would be so strong, so tall, that its permanence would be irrefutable.

I couldn't give him something so permanent. Not here, not now. I would have to give him something different: the joy of something momentary.

Sunrise, heartbeat.
Sunrise, heartbeat.
I didn't wake him, but I was ready when he woke up.
Sunrise,
The sky was the color of pink lemonade. I couldn't see the sun, but I knew it was coming. He squeezed his eyes

closed a little tighter before opening them. He blinked away the blur, stretched in the sleeping bag, pressed against me. heartbeat.

I kissed his forehead, his eyelids, his cheek, his lips, his neck. I held his hand, then pressed it against my chest.

"Happy birthday," I said quietly.

And we stayed like that. On our backs, looking skyward. Listening as the world woke up. Tents unzipping, people yawning and groaning and saying good morning. Children crying out for breakfast, parents using their placating voices. Birds speaking to one another, wondering what was going on. Green banners rippling in the breeze. Footsteps, music. We couldn't see any of it—nothing but the blue of the sky emerging from the pink.

My heartbeat: steady, unrushed.

The two of us: awake in the pause, enjoying the ordinary within the extraordinary, each moment only slightly different from the last. My thoughts drifting to him. His thoughts drifting to me.

Momentary, permanent.

Permanent, momentary.

My birthday present: the ease of the day. This small stop. The beat that keeps me going.

We could've stayed there for minutes or for hours. The point was: Time didn't matter. Only our bodies, our breath. Only us.

And we stayed there, listening.

twenty-one

Then, a voice. Stein's voice.

"I'm sorry to wake you, but I wanted to let you all know how much I appreciate how many of you have stayed and how many of you have joined us over the last twelve hours. Your message is being heard, loud and clear. I hear it, my opponent hears it, the better angels around the governor of Kansas hear it, and America hears it. There are well over a million of you here and over five million of you at state capitols around the nation. Also, over twenty million of you have posted your names on our site to offer support. We will start showing those names on the screen to my left, just to let you all know that you don't just stand here in Kansas for yourselves, but you do so on behalf of countless others.

"It has been, as you can imagine, a long, long night for many of us. The governor of this state would prefer that we not be here.

He would like us to pack up and go home, so he can try to steal this election without any scrutiny. Members of the opposition party have told me to let the process take its course. If I don't like the results, they say, I can always take it to the Supreme Court. Well, I have to tell you: As far as I'm concerned, this is part of the process. I am not going to wait, I am not going to rely on others to make my case, and I am not going to silence my own voice or the collective voice of the people who voted for me. I am not going to shut my eyes and hope it goes away. There have been popularly elected Presidents who came before me who did not take to the streets when their elections were challenged . . . and these Presidents always lost the Presidency they deserved. In 2000, we all sat there holding our breath when we should have been yelling. In 2008 we got back power, but we didn't use any of that power to change the biased electoral system that prevents this country from being a true democracy, where one person's vote is worth just as much as any others. And after what happened in 2016, we saw people pour into the streets . . . but that was on Inauguration Day, not Election Day. Then in 2020 we had the people who lost fair and square, who didn't have any numbers on their side, claim they were victims. And people who should have known better went along with it, just because they thought they could get something out of it, no matter if they were subverting the very liberty they said they were trying to protect. Heck, we can even go back to 1877, when Tilden was robbed of the Presidency because racists made a deal with Hayes. Everyone's got an agenda . . . but none of those agendas should matter once we know who has the greatest number of votes.

"I owe it to my voters, to my country, to our democracy, and to my faith in justice to actively and forcefully defeat any efforts that seek to undermine the results of this election and the will of the people. I will be here for as long as that takes . . . and I thank you for joining me."

We were told that Stein would return to the stage once an hour, every hour, until the governor of Kansas backed down. In between his appearances, various other politicians and entertainers came onstage to rally us on. First up was a folksinger from the nineties—a favorite of Mira and Keisha's—who came armed with little more than her voice, a guitar, and some carefully chosen words. The song she sang was one I'd always thought of as a breakup song. But now I realized it was a protest song as well.

The houses have been condemned on Memory Lane
I'm tired of this struggle that leaves everything the same
I've tried so hard to make it work
that I'm dying inside
Well, you can take my past
But you can't have my tomorrow

Promises that remain promises are useless over time
I wish I could put a price on words
so you'd have to think before you spent them

I put so much faith in you
I lost all my faith in me
Well, you can take my past
But you can't have my tomorrow

I'm giving up on giving up
I can't leave it all to prayer
'Cause the first step to getting better
is knowing what's not there

You said you'd make it better
and that just makes it worse
Well, you can take my past
But you can't have my tomorrow

Yes, I want my life to last
So you can't have my tomorrow
No, you can't have my tomorrow

Jimmy and I lay listening from our sleeping bags. Then, when the folksinger was through, I unclasped his hand so we could both applaud.

"What are you thinking?" Jimmy asked.

Ordinarily, I hated this question because it felt invasive, like, hey, if I wanted you to know what I was thinking, I'd be saying it. But the truth right now was simple:

"I'm thinking about the song?"

"And what are you thinking about the song?"

"I'm thinking that for years I heard it one way, and now I'm hearing it a different way, and the difference is that now it's political."

I stopped there, but Jimmy said, "Go on."

"I don't know, it's just the whole way we're taught politics is wrong, isn't it? We're told it's a system, and that it isn't personal at all. *Activism* is personal. But *politics* . . . no, that's something above being personal. But at the end of the day, all politics is about is whether you care more about yourself than other people, or if you care about other people as much as you care about yourself. That's it. It's that simple."

Jimmy sighed. "Of course politics are personal. Any kid born Black or brown knows that from the start. And any queer kid knows that as soon as they figure out that they're different."

"I know. But I guess what the song made me think about is how when you're dating someone who doesn't have your interests at heart, you have to stop dating them . . . and when you're living in a country where the leaders don't have your interests at heart, you've got to break up with them, too."

"Which is why we're here."

"Yes."

Jimmy nodded, like he already knew all this. And he probably did.

"And you know what?" I said.

"What?"

"You can have my tomorrow, if you want it."

"I can think of no better birthday present than your tomorrow. And now, let me give you my today."

We were ready to jump back into the world.

twenty-two

Janna and Mandy's present was blueberry pancakes. This in itself would have been sweet, but even sweeter was the collective effort that went into making them. Since all the nearby grocery stores had been pretty much cleaned out, Janna and Mandy hadn't just made the pancakes from scratch; they'd also had to dredge up the ingredients from scratch. All they had, at first, were the blueberries, which Janna had packed from home, knowing they were Jimmy's favorite. So they'd started talking to our neighbors. Janna and Mandy and Sue and Elwood and Flora and Keisha and Mira moved from blanket to blanket, tent to tent, finding flour in one spot, eggs in another, cooking oil in a third. The pug owners behind us had brought along an electric griddle, which they let Elwood borrow. In return, we gave away some of our Everything Bars—but mostly people didn't ask for anything in return. They were happy to help out with a birthday present.

Jimmy enjoyed it thoroughly.

The only members of our group who didn't join us for breakfast were Gus and Glen, who remained in their tent even as the rest of the rally bustled into life. I imagined they were rallying in a different way . . . but when Gus finally emerged, he wasn't cheerful. Instead of looking peachy, he looked like the pits.

"Uh-oh," I murmured to Jimmy.

"Oh, not again," he murmured back.

As Glen came out of the tent and made his way to his brothers, Gus trudged over to us.

"What happened?" I asked.

"Oh, it's just so *everything*," Gus replied with a sigh. "I mean, he's super hot and he has good teeth, but when we were just us, you know, he didn't really play the hits. The oomph and ahhh were praiseworthy, but the chatter was mucho ungood. I mean, he said he loved how surface I was, and I know it was meant as a compliment, but . . . meh. Plus plus plus we totally couldn't sleep right—parts of us kept falling asleep before the rest of us did, you know? I just don't think it's going to work."

"Another soul mate bites the dust," Jimmy said.

"So much for love," Gus agreed. "So much for moon-star-sun-aligning knock-your-socks-off-through-your-shoes I'm-so-lucky-I-found-you kismet kissing-grinding love love

love. I'm just another sad refrain in an endless Taylor Swift song. Now, where are the pancakes?"

Somehow I knew Gus was going to be okay.

Glen, too, looked like he was going to be all right. Until I realized that the brother coming over to talk to Virgil wasn't Glen. It was Gary. Or maybe Ross.

"We should probably head home," he said. "But we wanted to thank you for giving us a ride."

Virgil shot a chastening look Gus's way. (Gus, forking pancakes onto his plate, didn't notice.)

"You don't need to let some derailed hanky-panky get in the way of your protest," Virgil told Gary (or Ross).

"No, sir. It's just that my brother has a game he has to get back for, and we didn't really plan to be here this long. I think the crowd is big enough that the three of us won't be missed."

I couldn't figure out if the *won't be missed* was directed at Gus or not. Ross/Gary didn't sound too bitter; if anything, he sounded genuinely thankful for the ride and the company . . . until Virgil's observation left him without anything else to say.

As we watched the triplets leave, Gus looked particularly bummed. But I think the rest of us were a little bummed, too—this was the first departure from our group, and it meant that other departures were also possible.

We all sat together at the center of our makeshift campsite. Hundreds of names scrolled across the screens each minute—the names of all the people who were with us even though they couldn't be with us, who had texted in to add weight to what we were doing. In the background, politicians tried to rouse us with their oratory, and musicians tried to engage us with their songs. We were focused, for the moment, on smaller things, like our lives.

"That's the problem with triplets," Gus said between bites. "You always wonder whether you went with the right one."

"Oh, that's not just with triplets," Jimmy chimed in.

I put down my fork. "What's that supposed to mean?" I asked, trying to play at making it sound playful.

"Nothing. I wasn't talking about us," Jimmy assured me. "And anyway, it's my birthday. You're not allowed to be angry with me."

"Maybe you've mistaken me for one of my identical twins," I said.

"Nah. I'd know you with my eyes closed."

Gus was starting to squirm. "Hey now, hey now," he said. "We're in a no-bickering zone, comprende?"

"We're not bickering," Jimmy and I said at the same time.

"Well, as long as the two of you agree on that . . ."

Jimmy thanked everyone for the effort behind the pancakes. We cleared off the plates, returned what needed to be returned, and then . . . sat. And listened. And waited. As promised, Stein came and spoke every hour on the hour. There wasn't much new to report—more election officials were coming out against the governor, but he was standing firm. Almost two million people were now in Topeka, but nobody knew what that would really mean. We were prepared to stay, but we weren't entirely prepared to have nothing to do but cheer and applaud and dig in our heels.

It was . . . a little boring.

Jimmy surprised me by being the one to ask Virgil about this.

"Don't get me wrong—I'm all for being a part of this," he prefaced. "But, Virgil, I'm just wondering what good it does to have us here. I mean, the governor of Kansas isn't going to back down just because we're in his town, right? We can't really change his mind, can we? Or intimidate him. So why, really, are we going to stay here?"

Mrs. Everett clucked her tongue a little, but Virgil was game to answer.

"All those people who are coming forward with information about the governor," he said, "where do you think they're finding the strength to come forward? Our man Stein—what do you think is giving him the strength to fight this instead of sending in all the lawyers? All the people who are at the state capitols—why do you think they're staying put? It's because of us. Every single one of us. As one great mass, we're doing something presidents and kings and queens and governors and mayors and teachers and parents are supposed to do: We're leading by example. I agree that the governor is probably too stubborn a man to back down just because we're here. But it's because we're here that the right things are going to happen. It's because we're here that injustice will not win. Because they know we're watching. They know we won't just go along with whatever they try to do to us. They weren't expecting a fight like this, but by golly they've gotten a fight. And in that case, there's strength in numbers, and a lot of that strength comes *from* the numbers. We lead by example, the truth's gonna be helped. Just watch. If we leave, then they think they've won, and that means they think they can keep doing whatever they can to win, even if the numbers aren't there. We're not gonna let them think that. Because, thank goodness, it ain't true. We get up, stand up for our rights. We *won't* give up the fight."

As soon as he finished, a roar began to spread through the crowd. Green banners were held aloft and flown. Teenagers jumped up and down. Janna and Mandy shrieked. I thought I even saw one pug owner cry.

Much to my horror, Holy Ghostwriter was taking the stage.

twenty-three

All revolutions have to have music. It's rarely noted in the documents and organizations that follow—the Declaration of Independence doesn't have a tune; to my knowledge, the United Nations doesn't have a theme song.

Revolutionary music is never really what you'd expect. Take, for instance, the flute. Who would ever expect revolutionary fervor to come out of a flute? But right there next to the little drummer kids, you'll usually find a flute larking like the voice of better times, of innocence made to suffer for the greater good.

Or the trumpet, which can be so full of mourning and jazz, rouses itself into a *Glory, Glory, Hallelujah!* with one great blast of breath.

Holy Ghostwriter didn't have any flutes or trumpets. In fact, there were many people (myself and Jimmy included) who doubted its members played any instruments at all. But still, the minute Abraham Stein said their name, they received an orchestral response.

"We're here," Apostle, the lead singer, said, "because we believe that good must triumph over evil. Even though Stein is not of our faith, he is still a man of faith, and we have faith in that. I've been up all night writing this song for you. It's not much, but I hope it sums up why we're all here, and the nation we want to see. It's called '4 the Future.'" (We knew it was *4* and not *for* because Apostle held up four fingers as he said the word.)

Apostle nodded, and suddenly there was a blast of sound as harmonic as it was loud—a euphony of synthesizer and string. Apostle nodded as it amplified over us, stretching his arms out wide. Then he returned the microphone to his lips and began to sing his anthem.

U R 4 Me
And I M 4 U
That is what
He'd want us 2 do

Love 1 another
It's what we're here 4
2 True 2 B 4-gotten
He does not ask 4 more

U R 4 Me
And I M 4 U

Brothers and sisters
We'll see this thru. . . .

By the third time Apostle repeated it, everyone was singing along. I felt absolutely ridiculous, but when Janna reached for my hand and everyone else started to hold hands and sing out the words, I couldn't deny what was happening. The word I thought was *united*. How powerful it was to be in a country whose key adjective is *united*. How strong to be in a moment where everyone felt *united*.

Janna and Mandy looked rapturous with every chord, while Jimmy (on the other side of me, holding my other hand) looked like he was about to rupture from holding his laughter in.

I leaned into him and said, "Hey, you could take it a little more seriously."

"I love it."

"Well, then, I have a confession to make."

His eyebrow rose. "Yes?"

"This is your birthday present."

"Holy Ghostwriter?"

"Yes. You would not believe the things I had to do in order to get them here to sing for you—or, should I say, 4 U?—on your birthday."

"What did you have to do?"

"I can't tell you everything. But sexual favors were definitely involved."

"You slept with the members of Holy Ghostwriter?"

"The members and their members. Yes."

"Even Apostle?"

"Apostle twice. But one of them was for free, so that doesn't really count."

"U really do love me, don't U?"

"U R the 1 I'm living 4."

"U R 2 good 2 me."

"4 sure."

At this point, Janna yanked me away from Jimmy and told me to shush—Holy Ghostwriter was about to perform her favorite ballad, "1 + 1 is 3" ("1 + 1 is 3 / Because there's no love the Lord can't C / I'll gladly B / a part of your Trinity / Together U n' me / will make 1 + 1 into 3").

I let go of Janna's hand, Jimmy let go of Gus's, and we kissed like schoolgirls.

"You guys," Janna muttered.

"Sometimes music carries you forward; sometimes you get carried away," I said with a smile.

That was, I discovered, the good thing about a crowd: You didn't have to hold hands to be united. You just had to hold close.

Jimmy and I watched as Holy Ghostwriter continued to perform. Some screens were still showing the names of all the people supporting us from afar. Others showed the concert, and every now and then they'd pan across the crowd, showing all the faces underneath the green banners. Usually I couldn't care less about crowd shots, but this time was different, because I felt a connection to each and every face they showed.

Then the camera showed an attractive woman with night-black hair, inch-long eyelashes, and near-perfect cheekbones.

"That's my father!" Sue cried out. "That's the woman who's my daddy!"

twenty-four

Like a shot, Sue was picking up his things and heading off to find his father. We tried to figure out which part of the park she was standing in, but there weren't very many clues, and the camera cut away from her after a few more seconds.

"She must be near the front," Keisha said.

"Probably near the stage, since most of the cameras are up there," Mira agreed.

Some of us volunteered to go with him. But Sue said no, he wanted to do this alone. He took our numbers so he could call if he got lost. We showered him with encouraging words as he left.

"Kin always gravitates toward kin," Mrs. Everett observed.

"Do you have any kin here?" Flora asked sweetly.

"Why, no," Mrs. Everett replied, just as sweetly. "I consider y'all my kin."

Virgil just sighed and started humming the "U R 4 Me" song.

It wasn't long after Holy Ghostwriter exited the stage that Sara reappeared. As soon as she did, Keisha and Mira went careening in different directions.

"Wait," Sara said. "No. I have something to say to you both."

She looked like her thoughts hadn't slept at all since she'd left. Her hair, which had always been immaculately settled, was now haphazard and free. Her eyes had shadow both below and within. She closed them for a moment before speaking again.

Keisha and Mira hovered, waiting. We *all* waited to see what Sara would say next.

"You don't have to—" Flora started. But Sara waved her off.

"No, I want to do this. Since I seem to have dragged everyone into it, everyone might as well hear what I have to say. I want to apologize to you, Mira. And I want to apologize to you, Keisha. I should've known better than to do what I did. I should've been an adult. But I wasn't. And one of the things that's burning me the most is the thought that I've broken up the two of you. I know that doesn't make any sense. It doesn't make much sense to me, either. Except that it's true. I know this will sound strange, but I never meant to come between the two of you. I got caught up in everything—the campaign, the way we all are together, the sight of the two of you being so happy. I wanted a piece of that."

"What are you saying?" Mira challenged. "I don't understand what you're saying."

"I'm saying it was my fault. And if I could take it back, I would."

She didn't mean it. It was so obvious to me—she didn't mean it. She was doing this for Keisha.

How could I tell? Maybe it was the way she wasn't really looking at them. Maybe it was the way she seemed so much smaller than life. Maybe it was because I recognized the sound of someone still in love, since that was the way I talked, too.

She wasn't coming right out and saying she'd never loved Keisha. She couldn't betray everything. But at the same time, she was giving both of them an out—a way out of this mess and into a new beginning.

Finally, she looked at Mira. "I started it," Sara said. "I said all the right things because I knew they were the right things. She never intended to leave you. She was confused. She always loved you. The whole time, she loved you."

This was where Keisha could have denied it. This was where she could've told us all about being in love with two people at the same time.

But instead she stayed quiet. Said nothing. Let the story

stand. Because she had always loved Mira. And now Sara was stepping aside.

Sara turned to Clive and said, "I need the keys. I need to get my stuff. I'll get another ride back."

"I'll go with you," he said.

Sara shook her head. "No, I can do it alone. I'll call you when I'm back and I'll meet you to hand over the keys. I won't come back here."

When someone is hurting enough inside, you can see it on the outside—they hunch like a heart attack or grimace like a knife has just gone into their side. With Sara, it was as if her legs had become sticks—each step was its own effort, a teeter rather than a flow. But still she walked on, without looking back.

Keisha watched her go, then turned to Mira and said, "I guess we have to talk."

"Well, guess again," Mira said. Then they, too, walked away. Not so far, but far enough for the distance to be known.

"What do I do now?" Keisha asked us all.

No one had an answer.

Onstage, Alice Martinez quoted from Martin Luther King, Jr.:

"'Cowardice asks the question: Is it safe? Expediency asks the question: Is it politic? Vanity asks the question: Is it popular?

But conscience asks the question: Is it right? And there comes a time when one must take a position that is neither safe, nor politic, nor popular'—but you must take it because conscience tells you it is right."

It was colder today than it was yesterday. We began to feel it. And we began to feel hungry, and unwashed, and tired.

"I didn't think this would be easy," Gus said, "but I didn't think it would be so uncomfortable."

Jimmy's parents called, wishing him a happy birthday and telling him they were "holding down the fort" in Trenton, by the capitol building. They were there with dozens of their friends, and they were rotating their shifts so that some people got to drive home and sleep.

"I'm jealous," Jimmy admitted once he'd hung up.

I tried to comfort him with a back rub, but it only made him tense to have my cold hands against his back. Tense, until he got used to it.

We were listening to the news, waiting for some change. But it was the same news over and over, just as it was the same speech over and over from the stage.

"It's cool to be here," I reminded him.

"No, it's cold to be here," he corrected. "Damn Kansas."

I knew the trap we were about to fall into—Jimmy was becoming testy, which would make me anxious, which would make him even more testy, which would make me even more anxious . . . until our exasperation would boil over into outright mutual annoyance. I didn't want that to happen.

I tried to keep it light. "The weather isn't really Kansas's fault."

"Yeah, but the fact that we're here is."

I should have let it go, but I found myself saying, "The majority of Kansans voted for Stein. So it's not really their fault, either."

"Duncan, why are you defending *Kansas*?"

"I'm sorry. I know you weren't planning to spend your birthday in Kansas. I understand that's weird."

"I don't care about my birthday. *You're* the one who cares about my birthday."

"What does *that* mean?"

"Nothing. Never mind. This is stupid."

"Do you not want us to celebrate your birthday?"

"It just seems we should be focusing on the bigger picture right now."

"Jimmy, we're just standing here. That's all we're being asked to do. I think we can do that and celebrate your birthday at the same time."

"You don't have to. That's what I'm trying to tell you—you think you have to, but you don't."

But I want to! I wanted to say. I realized this would only prove whatever point he was making.

It was true: I cared about birthdays more than he did. I had always been like that, but it became even more intense during the pandemic. We tried all the workarounds—Zoom parties, or even parties where people would drive to our front yards and sing "Happy Birthday" from over six feet away. But it wasn't the same. Birthdays are meant to be the one day more than any other that you feel loved and appreciated. That was hard to convey under lockdown. So when lockdown lifted . . . I guess I wanted to compensate for the lost birthdays.

"Look," I said, "this isn't how I wanted it to be, either. But plans fall through. And if we've learned anything it's that you can't mourn lost plans. You just have to make new plans."

"Duncan, we're not on vacation."

"I am aware of that. Very aware of that."

I didn't like my own tone, the way my words were deployed for their bluntness. Jimmy hadn't made me anxious after all. We'd gone straight to annoyed.

I told him I was going to walk around with Elwood for a little bit.

He didn't invite himself along.

twenty-five

"Tell me about Passover," Elwood asked. We were just walking—no real destination in sight. I had one eye out for Sue; I was hoping he'd found his father but was sure that if he hadn't he'd still be around, searching.

"Passover? That's not until April."

"I know," Elwood said. "But I've never celebrated it. I can't wait to."

It's not that I hadn't given Passover much thought; the whole point of Passover was to give it thought. But I'd never tried to explain it before, especially to an aspiring Jew.

"Well, my whole family gathers for a seder. It's basically a big family meal, only you have a Haggadah to read from— it's basically the story of the exodus of the Jews from Egypt, and you retell it every year to remember what happened, like the fact that God parted the Red Sea and we escaped from the pharaoh."

"I know that part," Elwood said solemnly.

"Yup. But it's more than that. On Passover, we remember that no matter where we are in our lives and in the world, we were once slaves and we were once strangers. And because of that—because we were the victims of injustice—we must dedicate ourselves to fighting injustice, to fighting slavery, and to being kind to all strangers, for we ourselves were once strangers in a strange land. We end by saying, 'Next year in Jerusalem; next year may all be free!' And that means *everyone,* Jews and non-Jews. It's supposed to remind us that our goal is to make the world an ideal place, with peace and freedom for all."

"And you eat matzoh."

"Yes, we eat matzoh. Unleavened bread. Because the bread in the desert didn't have enough time to rise."

"I love matzoh."

I looked at Elwood. "When have you had matzoh?"

He blushed. "I snuck some. Is that okay?"

I smiled and told him I was sure it was okay.

I felt bad for Elwood, because I knew that when this was all over, he'd have to go back home and deal with whatever limitations lived there. But I also felt that clearly there was no way to keep the outside world away from him. Soon enough, when he was able to leave, he would get to live in that outside world and be whoever he wanted to be. It was no doubt frustrating to wait. But the wait would be worth it. We in the outside world would welcome him.

Still, I felt like I had to warn him. "You know it's not all holidays and celebrations, right? There are a lot of people out there who hate us, for no real reason other than they need someone to hate in order to feel things have been rigged against them. When I was a little kid, I didn't really understand that, because there were plenty of other Jewish kids around. I didn't feel different, except maybe when the world shifted over to Christmas. But in recent years, the threats have been so frequent, with neo-Nazis openly supported by the opposition party. Not the entire opposition party, but more of it than I ever would have imagined. So you have to be careful. Even the people who say they have love in their hearts can somehow make an exception when it comes to us."

"Hasn't it always been that way?"

"Yes, but I guess as the decades went by after the Holocaust, we started to believe again that we were safer. Not safe, but safer. The hate against us seemed more and more on the fringes, not as institutional. But then the deniers came along."

"The deniers?"

"It's the root of so many of our problems now, with the undermining of truth. The white supremacists started to deny that the Holocaust ever happened. They said it was a hoax. And then when the internet came along, suddenly they had this platform that they never would have had with leaflets or street corners. We're talking the death of twelve million people here, six million of them Jews. We're talking an event that was methodically recorded, with millions of eyewitnesses. And yet, there were people who felt they could erase it, simply by saying it wasn't true. And if you can erase the Holocaust through denial, what can't you erase? If the fact of so many people dying can be called into question, then what can't be called into question? At their heart, the Decents should really be called the Deniers. Because ultimately that's the power they want to wield. They want their fiction to become our fact. And even if most of them would say the Holocaust did in fact happen, they are also willing to rub elbows with the people who don't. They legitimize erasures that should never, ever be legitimized. And every time they do, we Jews are less safe. Because in the story the Decents are writing, we are not main characters. And they have no problem sacrificing minor characters if it means they get to stay in control. We can be thrown into the fire to fuel the hate machine at any time. I know that's dark. Believe me, it's not anything I want to be saying. But that's where we are. We have to be vigilant for ourselves and we have to be vigilant for everyone else the white supremacists want to erase."

"But you can't give up, because it's who you are."

"Yeah. That's right."

"History doesn't have to repeat."

"The only way to stop it from repeating is to change the way people see each other and treat each other. To be on guard in a way that our predecessors weren't able to be.

And we also have to live up to our own standards, which is something that doesn't always happen. We're no better than anyone else, but we're also no worse than anyone else. Does that lineage still interest you?"

"It does."

"Then maybe next year you'll go to Jerusalem."

"Yeah, maybe next year I'll go to Jerusalem," Elwood said.

"Stranger things have happened," I told him, knowing that when we say *Anything is possible,* what we really mean is: *I hope that good is possible.*

twenty-six

I wondered how long it would take the governor of Kansas to recount the votes. I wondered if he could really swing the election the other way. I wondered if the country could survive that, or if we'd go back to being brainwashed by products and the division into *us* vs. *them* and the daily microconflicts that the internet fed on.

I was impatient. If it was all going to go wrong, I wanted it to go wrong now. I wanted to know whether staying here would be worth it.

When Elwood and I got back, Jimmy had gone off with Virgil and Janna to wait on a long line at a local pizza place to get us something to eat. The news was changing from *Taking a Stand in Kansas* to *How Long Will They Last?* Even though trucks were arriving with food and supplies from around the country, it wasn't easy for them to get near the protests. Above us, clouds formed, and even though it didn't rain, it did get colder, and a lot of us weren't dressed for that. Even though we were surrounded by people and civilization, our bodies felt like we'd been out camping for a day too long, in need of a shower, a good mattress, and some central heat.

My mother called and asked when we'd be coming home. *I don't know* was not an acceptable answer, even though it was the only one I had. Elwood's parents had clued in and wanted him home, too. Mandy's mom was threatening to drive to Kansas herself to bring Mandy back.

"You need to go to school," my mom said, and when my dad got on the line, he echoed this. He said the principal had sent an email to parents saying that any election-related absences would still count as absences. And I had a feeling my parents would only be allowed to write so many sick notes . . . if they were willing to do that. I had the awful thought of Mr. Davis assigning quiz after quiz, just so he could fail us.

Then I imagined what Jimmy would say about where my thoughts were going: *Democracy is at stake and you're worried about your grades? C'mon, Duncan.*

I didn't even tell him about my parents' call when he got back with the pizza, about two hours after he'd left. He said the lines were epic, and that people were getting grumpy. Even though we were all on the same side, the resentments were growing. And the other side hadn't gone anywhere, either. If anything, they were shouting louder. Jimmy said there were police and National Guard everywhere, trying to keep everyone on their best behavior. Having the police and the National Guard walking around with their guns clear in sight only made people more tense.

Our group gathered around the pizza boxes as if they were a campfire. Janna made a pizza toast to Jimmy's birthday, and we raised our slices in salute. He smiled, but I could tell his heart wasn't in it. I wanted to ask him if he wanted to go home, but was afraid that even asking the question would seem disloyal. If he wanted to leave, he'd tell me. I was the one who kept things in.

When we sang "Happy Birthday," a lot of the people around us chimed in. It felt like group effort again. When Stein came out to talk to us, I half expected him to wish Jimmy a happy birthday, too. Instead he told us we were fighting the good fight, making good trouble, and that even though the process of justice was moving slowly, we were helping to sit on the scales to make sure it moved in the right direction.

Then, roughly ten minutes after he left the stage, news started to come in from Tallahassee.

You could see it spread through the crowd. People noticing something on their phones. Telling the people around them to take a look.

Then: shock and horror.

In our group it was Keisha who saw it first. She immediately called out to the rest of us to show what had happened. And there it was, contained by a screen but still right in front of us: the car driving into the crowd. The screams and falling bodies. The way it went on and on, until finally the car stopped and police surrounded it.

Then, more news. Another car attempting to drive into the crowds in Harrisburg. Calls for people not to panic. A man in Sacramento pulling out an AK-47 and firing it in the air. The chief of police in Topeka taking the stage, telling the millions of us to stay calm, that law enforcement was on high alert.

Everyone started getting phone calls. To make sure we were okay. To tell us to come home. I could tell from my mother's voice that she was crying, terrified. Even Jimmy's parents were upset, were wondering what was going to happen. He assured them we were okay, but he didn't take it one step further, saying it would all be okay.

I was shocked, but I was not surprised. I was horrified by what I was seeing unfold, but it also felt like forces had been unfolding such violence for years. Deep in my heart, I'd known something like this was going to happen.

After so many years of vitriol. After so many years of demonization and dehumanization. After so many years of conservative gatekeepers looking the other way as white supremacists and conspiracy theorists walked through the gates. After people in power told their followers that the truth was theirs to bend to their will. After people in power told their followers that they had to fight or be replaced. After months of voters being told by the other side that the election was going to be stolen from them. After all that . . . it felt inevitable that someone was once again going to drive a car into a crowd, killing whoever stood in their way. And then other people were going to copy this act.

We were told Stein would come out to address us in a matter of minutes. Part of me wanted to tell him not to, to tell him it was too risky. Who could say there wasn't a gunman in the crowd? How can you protect one man from a multitude that stretches millions?

He must have been afraid. It's human to be afraid when you know there are people who will stop at nothing to make you afraid.

Stein went onstage and told us violence was not the answer. We all chanted it after he said it.

Violence is not the answer.

Violence is not the answer.

Violence is not the answer.

Even as I said these words, I thought, *But violence has always been the question.* Not a distinctly American question, but certainly one that has bedeviled our country, the more so as it became easier to use a weapon to kill many people in an instant, without having to be at close range.

Stein called on the opposition candidate to condemn what had happened, but the opposition candidate couldn't bring himself to do it fully. He said the protests were an aggression, and that aggression incites aggression. He made himself the victim, because powerful people losing their power will always slide into the victimhood they deplore in people who are actually victimized by systems of power.

The governor of Kansas was more decisive, saying that no violence would be tolerated, declaring the entirety of the protest zone a weapon-free area. I didn't know how enforceable that was, but it was still good to hear. The governor was willing to take away our votes, but at least he didn't want us to be killed on his watch.

The news showed some people leaving, the crowd having more empty spaces. Not as many people were coming in to replace them. Stein made many announcements asking us all to stay where we were, to prevent the chaos of a mass exodus.

Virgil called an emergency meeting.

"I've been getting word from all your parents," he said. "They want us home, and they want us home now."

"So that's it?" Jimmy said. "We give up on peaceful protest the minute the other side uses violence? Is that what history teaches us, Virgil?"

Virgil shook his head. "I hear you, Jimmy. But at the end of the day, you're all still minors. And if your parents call you home, then I gotta bring you home."

"I can't believe you're saying that." Jimmy sounded disgusted.

"Don't take it out on him," Flora interrupted. "He's as heartbroken as you about this."

I thought Jimmy would relent, but his body remained

tense. I tried to put my hand on his shoulder, but right there, in front of everyone, he pulled away.

"Well," Janna said, "we can't leave until at least tomorrow. It's getting dark and they're telling everyone it's safer here than trying to get on the roads."

Virgil nodded. "That's what I told your parents, and they understand. The last thing they want is for us to be trying to press through the crowds in the dark. So hunker down . . . for our last night here."

Nobody was in the mood to celebrate anymore—not Jimmy's birthday, not our pride in being present. Instead we remained as glued to our phones as we could be with chargers in short supply, watching as the National Guard moved in to protect us, and as a few rogue truckers decided to express their views on our protest by stalling their vehicles on the main highways out of Topeka, snarling traffic further. It looked like we might not get out anytime soon. And instead of feeling like protesters, we were starting to feel like sitting ducks.

Stein and others came out to rally us, to tell us we were still fighting the good fight. Volunteers passed out water and food and blankets, because the night was supposed to dip well below freezing. The singers came on with their protest songs, but fewer of us were singing along.

I didn't really have a chance to talk to Jimmy alone until we were back in our sleeping spot. It was only nine, but we'd decided to call it a night. We half expected Virgil to get us up at sunrise to try to make an early retreat, if the roads were cleared and the conditions were right.

The breaking news kept breaking us. One of the victims in Tallahassee was a nine-year-old girl. Another car attempted to crash into the protest in Austin, but the police shot the driver before he could make it to the crowd. Hundreds of violent white supremacists were trying to circle the Supreme Court building in DC. The justices were supposedly under heightened guard.

I tried to remember it was Jimmy's birthday, and that I had to try to be extra nice to him. But I didn't know how to reconcile that with his anger.

"You can't take it out on Virgil," I told him, cuddling in to counter the cold. "It's not his fault."

"I know it's not his fault," he said. "Or our parents' fault. Or Stein's fault. It's this fucking country's fault."

"We're part of this country, too," I reminded him. "You can't define us by our worst elements."

Jimmy rounded on me then and said, "I can when they win! Don't you see, Duncan—they're going to win. Because they're willing to kill people. Because they're willing to wreck the truth. Because they don't care about anyone but themselves, and are willing to take us all down as collateral damage. Guess what: It's an effective strategy! Fear works!"

I didn't like seeing Jimmy like this. I hadn't really seen it before, this despair. It was unnerving because he was supposed to be the positive one, the optimist. I was supposed to be the cynic.

"We can't give up," I told him. "Not now. Not when we've come all this way. If we give up now, then they really do win. And if they win on their terms, then it's much worse than any single election."

"It doesn't matter," Jimmy said. "Can't you see . . . it doesn't matter."

"It does," I argued. "It has to."

"I'm telling you, they're going to win."

This was it. The abyss.

I had glimpsed it before. In my parents' haunted faces the morning after Trump won. In the early days of the pandemic, when we took shelter in our houses and didn't leave. When I wondered if every time one of my parents went to the grocery store they'd come back with something deadly. When the number of deaths built into a mountaintop. Then, the insurrection. Seeing the wild, uncontrollable crowd storm the Capitol, gleefully calling for politicians to be killed. Thinking: This is how the American experiment fails. This is how democracy and the safety of democracy get yanked from our hands. This is the breakage of our society. And all we'll have left is . . . the abyss. We will be toppled by our own greed. We will be toppled by our lust for violence. We will be toppled by the fuel of hate added to the fires of resentment. The danger was always there in front of our eyes. But we chose to look away, at our entertainments.

We ceded responsibility so we could shop and argue with our neighbors. The abyss was always there; we just build more entrances.

America is a lie, but it's a useful one. It's something we can work toward instead of the abyss.

Those in power liked to think our system was safer, better than others. We had staved off the chaos of other societies, the warfare. But all along we'd been much closer to crossing that line than we'd thought. And that "safer, better" had only applied to the majority all along.

I didn't think I had the strength to pull Jimmy from the abyss, but I had to try. I knew I didn't have the strength to pull America from the brink of the abyss, but I had to try.

"No," I said to him, making sure he was looking at me, that we were seeing each other clearly. "They're not going to win. Because most Americans are like us. They don't want to plunge into the abyss. They don't want people shooting up stores or schools or nightclubs. They want elections to be won by the person with the most votes. They don't want crimes to go unpunished and lies to go uncorrected. They don't like politics and politicians, but they like entropy even less. They want security, not insecurity. They want peace of mind, not fear. We are the majority. For the past four presidential elections, we have been the majority. But voting aside—most people want to live by love, whether it's God's love or love for each other or both. They want to leave the world better than when they got here. They want the future to be better for the next generations. They don't want another civil war."

"Then why are we here? Why does this keep happening?"

"We are here because we need to make our principles visible. The other question has thousands of individual answers. Every person who allies with the abyss has their own story, because selfishness is always part of the equation. But the antidote to that is one story, and that's the story we're here to defend."

Jimmy was shaking now. From fear, or sadness, or anger, or maybe that overwhelming wave when all of them meet. I held him, and he held me back, and that was how we built the life raft, that was how we resolved everything we knew we couldn't resolve. We stepped back from the abyss, into the mundane. So we could find a way to sleep. So we could find a way to face the morning.

twenty-seven

Shortly after we woke up and got the lay of the land, it became clear we weren't going anywhere.

Not only was there trouble on the highways going out of Topeka, but people had begun to come back in again. In the wake of Tallahassee, a new group of people had been energized to join us, to condemn the violence and aggression.

Jimmy's spirits seemed to have thawed a little.

"Wanna go on a supply run to the bus?" he asked me. "We're going to go and get the rest of the food."

"Whatever you want, Belated Birthday Boy," I answered.

"I suppose a Holy Ghostwriter encore is out of the question?"

"You mean you want me to put out again?"

"Only if it wouldn't put U out."

I swatted at him, and he swatted at me.

"Bickering!" Gus called out.

"It's not bickering!" we shouted back.

Janna, Mandy, Clive, and Virgil were going to come along with us. As we headed out, the new level of security was clear—not just in the presence of countless police officers and National Guardspeople, but also in the wary expression of people as we passed. I didn't think we looked at all suspicious, and once people focused on us, we usually got smiles or nods. But at first, when we were just motion-sensed on the side, there was an initial tenseness, a layer of worry.

"We're leaving Mira and Keisha in the same place at the same time?" I asked Jimmy, trying to make the walk as conversational as possible. "Have you seen any signs of reconciliation?"

Jimmy shook his head. "Nope. But do you really think there should be?"

The rest of our group was ahead of us. It was just the two of us talking.

"You don't?" I asked.

He paused. We were approaching the counterprotesters. The security was particularly intense around them, and it looked like they hadn't been given much leeway in leaving their enclosure. They were looking bedraggled—as hungry, cold, and unwashed as we were. Their shouting wasn't as loud now, but the edge in it was sharper. The police weren't there to prevent them from insulting us, just from shooting us.

We tried to ignore it.

"Don't you want them to get back together?" I pressed.

"Honestly, I don't know. I mean, what Keisha did was pretty rotten, no matter what Sara says. How can Mira ever trust her again?"

"But if she's sorry, doesn't that matter?"

We weren't talking about us, but with any couple, whenever you talk about another couple it becomes at least partly a conversation about your own relationship.

"If Keisha's so sorry, she shouldn't have been making out with Sara," Jimmy said. I wasn't crazy about the judgment in his voice . . . but then I thought, *If it had been Jimmy with Sara, wouldn't I be saying the same thing?*

It was so complicated. I wanted forgiveness from Jimmy, even though it wasn't for me.

Once we were closer to the bus, Janna ducked back to us.

"Did you see those Decents protesting?" she asked. "They weren't in good shape."

"Maybe that means they'll leave," Jimmy said. "We can hope."

I didn't disagree with that. It would have been satisfying to outlast them.

We looked ahead to Virgil, Mandy, and Clive. They seemed to be studying something on the bus. When we caught up with them, we saw what they were looking at—eggs had been hurled at the bus's windows and sides.

"Waste of good food," Virgil said.

Janna stuck her finger in one of the egg spots. "This is a fresh assault. We could still make an omelet if we hurry."

We took a look at the other side of the bus, but apparently this side—the one with Gus's words on it—had been the only object of attack. I felt a little strange—what if the eggsailants were still close by? What if they chose another food group to attack us with?

I think my uneasiness was shared, since we moved with much more efficiency and much less talk than we had the day before. We unloaded the last boxes of food and a few extra blankets we'd taken. Then we locked up and started heading back—although not before each of us had used the bus's restroom. It wasn't spacious, but it was still a sight cleaner than the toilet cubes that had been set up around Topeka. We also convinced Clive to run the engine a little so we could charge our phones.

"All right," Virgil said when the last of us was finished. "Let's beat it."

As we started back downtown, Clive said to Jimmy, "I bet this isn't how you pictured your birthday week would go."

Jimmy looked over to me, like I'd put Clive up to saying it. Mandy jumped in and asked Virgil what his weirdest birthday ever was, and he told us a story involving a surprise party, an abandoned car wash, a Buick, and Flora with a nest of cherries in her hair.

It was good to be laughing, as all of us were. All of us except Janna, who seemed to have something else on her mind.

It was only when we got to the counterprotesters that we found out what it was.

twenty-eight

"We need to help them," Janna said.

I knew exactly who she meant, but even Mandy was a little confused.

"Who?" they asked.

"Them." Janna pointed to the ragged bunch of screamers that we were approaching, their posters a little worn but still full of poisoned words. "Look at those kids on the side. I wonder if they've had anything to eat the past two days. We should offer them some of the energy bars we have. We have plenty, especially with the triplets and Sue gone. We should share. It's what Jesus would want us to do."

I was in no position to argue what Jesus would or wouldn't want.

"Really, Janna," Jimmy said, "I think that's too much. We can share with the people around us at the rally. Our side."

"No. Look at them." Sure enough, there were a bunch of kids at the edge of the counterprotest, looking like they missed home in a big way. A camera crew was nearby, asking an adult to spite-spew for the news.

But Janna wouldn't relent. "Luke, chapter six, verses thirty-five and thirty-six," she said. " 'Love your opponents, do good to them, and give to them without expecting to get anything back. Then your reward will be great, and you will be children of the Most High, because God is kind to the ungrateful and cruel. Be merciful, just as God is merciful.' That's what 'U R 4 Me and I M 4 U' is all about."

" 'U R 4 Me and I M 4 U'?" This time Jimmy didn't hold back his laugh. "How about, 'They R Not 4 Us, So We Should Give Our Food 2 People Who R'? They're running cars into us—surely that's a disqualifier."

"I don't see any of those kids driving cars. Or carrying weapons."

"Not yet."

"Why don't we vote?" Janna asked. "All in favor?"

Janna and Mandy raised their hands. And Virgil. And Clive. And me.

"Against?"

Jimmy didn't bother to raise his hand.

"C'mon," Mandy said.

"No—you go ahead." Jimmy held up his hands in surrender. "I'm not going to do it with you. I'm going to walk past them and have them tell me I'm going to hell and that

I'm a dirty Black fag who deserves to die. You can go break bread with them."

I saw his point. Really, I did. It's just that I saw Janna's point more.

"Jimmy," I said. I wanted him to stay. I desperately wanted him to stay. Partly because that would mean he didn't think I was wrong.

"Do what you want, Dunc," he replied, shutting me down.

Virgil started to say something then, but Jimmy was already leaving. I started to follow, but Virgil told me, "Let him go."

And I did.

I don't think they saw us. Not the adults, at least. But the kids knew something was up. There were about ten of them, and none of them was over eight. Janna got to them first. "Here," she said, handing a little girl an energy bar. "It's the chocolate kind."

The bar hadn't even gotten into the girl's hand when a voice suddenly shouted out, "What do you think you're doing?"

It happened so quickly.

Virgil trying to explain.

Janna and Mandy handing out the food. Me and Clive holding the boxes.

Then all this shouting. Adults storming over. Yelling.

The kids taking the bars. Then the adults knocking them out of their hands. Reaching for Janna. Grabbing them out of her hands. Throwing them back at her.

Shouting. Spitting.

Virgil stepping in. Getting shoved.

This getting the attention of the police. Them shouting at all of us.

And the light. Suddenly there was more light than the declining afternoon deserved.

The camera lights. As soon as they were lit, the shouting became screaming, the shoves became harder.

I didn't know what to do. I clutched at the box.

Janna and Mandy were screaming now. A different kind of screaming. Not an attack. The opposite.

"Let me go. Let her go!"

I dropped my box. Other people were coming now. Passersby.

We stepped into the crowd as they broke their lines.

Police raising their guns. People not hearing.

Virgil was being hit. Hit in the chest and hit with the most vile words.

I got to Janna. Mandy. Put my arms around them and pulled them back into me.

Then the police were pushing us. Pushing us away. Trampling over the boxes, the food.

Kids crying. Adults throwing posters in our faces.

Other people—not just police—running in now to push them back.

Fights breaking out.

Fists. Blood.

"Lord!"

Virgil.

I watched as he came stumbling out, Clive supporting him.

Hurt. Not bleeding.

I thought it might be a heart attack.

"Are you okay? Are you okay?" I kept asking.

He nodded. He didn't look okay.

"Just shaken," he said.

There were people from the other side trying to hold the attackers back. Trying to comfort the children. Yelling at the ones who had gotten to Janna and Mandy.

They're not all bad, I had to remind myself.

I only half believed it.

The fighting continued until the police had pulled both sides apart. Separated us again.

"Well," Virgil said to Janna, "nobody ever said Jesus had it easy."

The cameras kept rolling.

Was Ludlow Rogers watching his screen, and did he see the girl being attacked on her mission of kindness? Had he been watching the crowds all day, knowing they were voting to stay, putting themselves on the line? Or was it simpler than that? Did he pray? Did he have to answer one of his children's questions about what was going on? Was it something that secretly he'd always known he'd have to do?

What was it about that moment that made him decide?

Whatever the case, some hours later, Ludlow Rogers made a phone call and pressed a button.

twenty-nine

Before I saw him, I heard Jimmy calling my name.

He had seen it. Later, we'd learn that everybody had seen it.

Janna reaching out with food.

And then.

And then.

One of the pug lovers had been watching as it was broadcast live. Breaking news. She said, "Something's happening," and everyone gathered around. Saw it as it happened. Saw it replayed. And replayed again.

Except for Jimmy. He didn't wait for the replay. He was already running.

*

"Duncan! Duncan!"

And then I saw him. There was a look on his face I had never seen before.

That fear.

That fear that comes from love.

When he saw me, it was as if his body released angels. He was so relieved. So afraid—because the fear doesn't wear off in an instant—and so relieved.

I have never been happier to see anybody.

He ran over to me, and he didn't need to say a thing. But he said so many things anyway—one long rush of "I'msorry areyouokayohmyGodI'msosorryIleftyouiseveryoneallright letmemakesureyou'reokayIwassoscaredIcameasfastasIcould I'msosorryIleftyouI'msosorryI'msohappyyou're okay."

I held him as he tried to hold me. As Virgil held Janna and Mandy. As the violence of the situation subsided into aftershocks. As we slowly, slowly followed Elwood back to the fifty square feet we thought of as our temporary home.

Mira and Keisha were waiting for us together. Holding hands because they needed to.

Gus was with a cute boy who also looked concerned. His name was Pierre. He was from France.

Flora had wanted to come looking for us, too. But Mrs. Everett had kept her close, saying, "They'll come back. Don't worry—they'll come back. If he comes back and you're not here, it'll only make it harder."

Flora kept shaking her head, asking the sky, "Why does it always come to this?"

I called my parents. We all called our parents.

Even though it was nowhere near the top of the hour, Stein came out to speak.

"As many of you have no doubt seen or heard, minutes ago there was a violent incident in which a group of kind, charitable youth were attacked by people who support my opponent. I am sure this is not something my opponent would condone, and it is certainly not something I condone. I know that seeing this attack may anger some of you, leading to more violence.

"Let me remind you all: We are here as nonviolent protesters, and we expect our opposition to follow the same rules. As Gandhi said, 'We must be the change we wish to see.' We will all adhere to that.

"I know you are cold. I know you are hungry. We are doing everything in our power to bring more blankets and more food to the area. In our great challenge, we face everyday challenges as well. The only answer I can give you is this: The more kindness and justice are challenged, the more we must embrace them. Only when you are challenged—and only when you challenge yourself—do you discover what truly matters. Your actions are being witnessed and your words are being seen—not just in

this city or state, but in this nation and the entire world. Stay strong. Morally strong. Spiritually strong. And physically strong. There is a Yiddish proverb that says, 'He that can't endure the bad will not live to see the good.' I promise you, we will get to the right end, and we will do it as quickly as possible."

Night fell.

thirty

Sue and his father found us, and they brought a camp-fire with them.

The resemblance was amazing, not just in their features, but in the happiness they so clearly felt in finding each other again. Sue's father was a gorgeous woman, and she spoke in a rich, robust voice. As we laid down the wood and lit it up, she told us stories—of her wandering days, of all the time she lost to drink, of the moment she knew she had to live as the woman she knew herself to be.

"We talk all the time 'bout hard truths," she told us. "But I reckon to tell you there are soft truths, too. It doesn't always have to be like running into a wall. Sometimes it's just like waking up."

Her one regret, she said, was leaving Sue behind.

"I always knew where he was," she said. "I just wasn't sure he'd want to have anything to do with a pa like me."

Sue just leaned into her in response. His father wiped a tear from her eye.

All through the story, Jimmy kept my hand in his. After, Janna and Mandy sang some gospel, and Mrs. Everett stood up to tell us how mighty we were. Gus and his new French boy flirted dreamily while Mira and Keisha had once again drifted apart—even though their glances kept colliding.

Eventually, Jimmy moved his mouth to my ear and said, "I'm sleepy."

"Let's go, then," I whispered. We said a full round of good nights, called our parents, got ready for bed, then slipped into our sleeping bag.

The fire was still burning behind us. The green banners still glowed. The night air wasn't really dark at all. It was a blue hour.

His face was mere inches from mine. His eyes were observing. He ran his hand behind my ear, down my neck. He kissed me gently. I kissed him gently back.

"I love you," he said.

"I love you," I said.

We lay there in a gentle equilibrium. Our knees touching. Our hands gliding. Quieter words. The slight heat of breath.

Gradually, very gradually, we fell asleep. Together.

*

The next morning, we heard the word before we knew what it meant. We woke up to it—people whispering it, speaking it, even exclaiming it.

recording. Recording. Recording!

We got up and looked at the news. We saw a man walking into an official-looking building.

His name, we learned, was Ludlow Rogers.

He was the governor of Kansas's chief of staff.

Recording.

"They say he made a recording of the governor," Virgil told us as we gathered around. "They say it could be something."

It was something.

Stein was late for his hourly speech. When he reached the stage, all he said was:

"I want you to hear something."

The governor's unmistakable voice trying to calm the opposition candidate.

The opposition candidate saying, "I don't care how we

do this, but we're going to do this. This state's not going to go for that Jew fag Stein—I don't care if I have to vote a thousand times myself to get the margin in our favor. We're almost there. The woman in Ford County's almost done."

That "woman in Ford County" was an election official. And she wasn't very happy about what the candidate had said.

The truth was emerging.

We were energized. By the millions, we were energized.

The chanting began. All of us in unison. All our voices, united.

What do we want?

Justice!

When do we want it?

Now!

And

We won Kansas! We won Kansas! We won Kansas!

And

Stein. Is. President!

Stein. Is. President!

Simple slogans. Irrefutable truth.

*

"I'm afraid to get my hopes up," Jimmy confided in me.

"Me too," I said. Because life doesn't play fair. In order to have faith in fairness, it requires hope.

Standing next to him, I felt a weird fast-forward—I was living the moment but I was also imagining telling someone younger than me about what it was like to be in this moment.

I took Jimmy's hand, and I could tell he was grateful for it, as grateful as I was. This seemed like the best way to approach the moment—with guarded hope, and with gratitude.

"I'm so glad we're here," I told him.

"I'm so glad we're here, too," he replied.

Together, we waited.

Not passively. Actively.

We yelled for hours. We filled the air with our protest. Nobody was leaving now. Not when we were so close.

More and more people joined us.

We would push it and push it and push it. We would push it until we got there.

"This is what democracy sounds like.

"This is what democracy looks like.

"This is what democracy is."

We forgot that we were cold. We forgot that we were hungry. We forgot that we were wearing yesterday's clothes, if not the clothes from the day before. We forgot any of the dramas that existed among us. We forgot any other conflicts.

"I know the one thing we did right
Was the day we started to fight
Keep your eyes on the prize
Hold on, my Lord, hold on!"
United.
We stood.

"Hold on," Stein told us. "Hold on."

We held hands. We kept going.
We hoped.

I thought about my great-grandparents, and what they'd think of a Jewish President. I thought about all the gay men who had not lived to see this day.

Suddenly, around two in the afternoon, the face of the governor of Kansas filled all the screens, including the one on the stage. We were confused—was this sabotage? Had his team somehow managed to jam Stein's broadcast and infiltrate our rally?

We looked to the stage.

Stein was nowhere to be found.

What was happening?

The news showed the opposition candidate.

He looked grave.

Solemn.

Defeated.

But also defiant.

The channels cut to the governor of Kansas.

He looked exhausted.

Disbelief swirled, carrying an undercurrent of joy.

Could it be?

Was it really?

We quieted. The governor began to speak.

We listened.

And then we began to cheer and weep.

"I have just spoken to Abraham Stein, as well as my staff, my wife, and my Lord. When this recount began, it was something I firmly believed in. But now I can no longer let it tear at the fabric of our country, not when I know it was begun in bad faith and conducted erroneously. It would be easy for me to dig in and to refuse the inevitable in order to save face; that, I fear, is the tradition I have been taught over many years in politics. But I started my career in order to do right by the greater good. And it is for the greater good, and for the tenets of truth and democracy, that I must say without equivocation that Abraham

Stein has rightfully won the state of Kansas, and therefore the Presidency of the United States. Let this be a moment when we all come together. . . ."

We'd done it.

Jimmy and I hugged each other so tight. We kissed. Then we jumped around with the rest of our friends—hugging them, hugging strangers, cheering loud into the sky.

"Hallelujah!" Virgil cried. "Hallelujah!"

Amen, I thought. *Amen.*

I have never heard such a noise as when Abraham Stein stepped onto that stage, the first gay, the first Jew, to be elected President of the United States.

Imagine the brightest colors possible. Then make them all into sounds. Then multiply that by two million voices.

That's what it sounded like.

We'd done it.

The Jesus Freaks and the gay kids. The old soldiers and the students who couldn't drive yet. Lovers and friends and exes and couples and female fathers. Every skin, every mix, every religion. People from Kansas and people from far beyond Kansas.

*

We'd done it. Because we had to. Because it was right.

There was a crowd standing behind Stein on the stage. Singers and actors. Ordinary volunteers. Alice Martinez. Stein's staff members. His husband. Their children.

And in front of them all—but not really separate from them—Abraham Stein.

He said:

"There are not words with which I can thank you all enough. Everyone on this stage with me. The millions of you standing in front of me and at the state capitols. The millions more of you who have supported me with your votes. I have been talking for over a year about building the Great Community. Now I have seen that part of the work has already been done. We are already together in so many ways.

"Your message is one that I have heard, loud and clear. And it is one that will guide me as I accept your trust and faith as the next President of the United States of America. We must be guided by our ideals, by our hopes of repairing the world, by our dedication to one another and to the principles of justice,

kindness, and compassion. We must stand up to evil, to fear, to hate. We must resist employing them as weapons in our own arsenal. We must remember that even though we are Americans, we are also citizens of the world and cohabitants of the earth. We must prize knowledge and creativity and invention. We must take care of one another.

"We must remember the preamble to our Declaration of Independence and usher in a new era of independence. We must remember the truths that our country is meant to hold as self-evident.

"Equality. No matter what our identity, we are considered equal in this nation.

"The unalienable right of life. That all of us are worthy and deserve protection from harm.

"The unalienable right of liberty. That all of us shall remain free.

"The unalienable right of the pursuit of happiness. Not just our own happiness, but the happiness of others as well. Do not just seek happiness for yourself. Seek happiness for all. Through kindness. Through mercy. Through opportunity.

"These are the most traditional values our country has ever had. They're in the document where it all began.

"The Declaration of Independence says that governments derive their just powers from the consent of the governed; that whenever any form of government becomes destructive of these ends, it is the right of the people to alter or to abolish it. We are not here out of rebellion but instead out of our own patriotic belief in America. We are not here to abolish our government, *but we are here to alter it back to its original ideas. We will no longer suffer disregard toward the well-being of our people, out of greed or war or hate. We will no longer try to pit the people against one another rather than inspire them to work together. The alteration we seek is one that returns us all to our unalienable rights and to the great democratic nation that this country can be.*

"Every single one of us must do what the signers of the Declaration did at the end of their document. We must mutually pledge to each other our lives, our fortunes, and our sacred honor. I pledge my life, my fortune, and my sacred honor to you, and thank you for the pledges you have made in return to me and to this country.

"This has been an astonishing moment for me, for my family, for everyone who has worked on this campaign, and for America. Thank you again for standing up for what is right. I look forward to seeing you all at our inauguration!"

thirty-one

We were there.

We had been there when he'd been elected. We had been there when his election was saved. So we were there in Washington, DC, when he was sworn into office.

Sue was there. With his father and his father's new boyfriend, Loretta.

Mrs. Everett was there. Flora had invited her to join us.

Sara was there. We saw her in the crowd and waved. She waved back, but she didn't stop to talk to us.

Virgil, Flora, and Clive were there. They'd driven us down, and we'd all sung "Amazing Grace" when we saw the Washington Monument in the distance.

Mira and Keisha were there. Mira was with their new girlfriend, Lisa. Keisha had just broken up with her new girlfriend, Jas. She still missed Mira.

Elwood wasn't there. But we used our phones to take him along with us, to show him what he was missing. I'd been taking him to synagogue that way, too. I'd been helping him with the Torah portion for his bar mitzvah.

Gus was there, with his new boyfriend, Ramón. They'd been going out for three days. This was a big deal.

("Whatever happened to Pierre?" I asked Gus, remembering our last day in Topeka. "Who?" he asked back.)

Mary Catherine was not there. Jesse Marin was not there. Mr. Davis was not there. We still had to deal with them at school, but they weren't as aggressive now. We tried to be nice to them.

Jimmy's parents were there. His whole family was—even, to our surprise, his conservative grandparents. ("I've never in my life been to an inauguration, and it's about time I went," his grandmother had said, and that was that.)

Janna and Mandy were there. They'd gone to church on Sunday, then had come straight down with us. They'd taken the Great Community to heart and were already using their church group to bring more people together—"To work for the greater good," Janna said. "Which is really what God's all about. A greater good."

Jimmy was there. Holding my hand so that our wrists touched, our pulses in tune. When we talked about the future now, we tried to find each other in it. Meanwhile, we enjoyed the present. We pursued happiness.

Stein walked up to the podium in front of the Capitol,

put his hand on the Hebrew Bible, and, with his beaming husband and impatient children at his side, became the President of the United States.

The thing that had once seemed impossible had not only become possible—it had become the foundation of everything that would come next.

I was there. Just one young gay Jew in a sea of people. Just one lone voice in an enormous body of sound. Just one unique person at one unique moment, there to witness something monumental.

I was a part of history.

We are all a part of history.

Author's Note and Acknowledgments

Wide Awake Now is a reimagining of my earlier novel *Wide Awake*. When I first started writing *Wide Awake* in 2004, I thought of it as a protest novel against the recently reelected administration of George W. Bush. I set it roughly twenty years in the future . . . which would take us to the election of 2024. My invented election of 2024 hinged on the highly contested results in a single state on the electoral map—it was meant to echo the election of 2000, but reading it today, the elections of 2016 and 2020 resonate even louder. And my fictional candidate's calls for fairness, justice, and unity to preserve democracy makes me sadder than I ever imagined they would when I wrote them twenty years ago.

So I decided to rewrite the book. Instead of an imagined 2024, I would set it in a real 2024—or, at least, an alternate 2024, where everything that's happened to us in the past twenty years has happened, but fictional candidates are running for President. I've gotten rid of a lot of the speculative details from the original, but the political speeches have remained almost entirely the same. It's just the context that's shifted.

I hope that in twenty years, this book already feels like a relic of a bygone era of hate, censorship, and divisiveness. As I'm writing this toward the end of 2023, there is a brutal movement trying to silence LGBTQIA+ and BIPOC voices—to put us back in the closet, to erase a true version of history for an old version of history. So many people are on the front lines of this battle for intellectual freedom that no acknowledgments section could possibly acknowledge them all; no dedication, except a very general one, could encompass my appreciation for defending our democracy against those who want to reshape it in their own image. I know the best I can do is to keep putting these stories out in the world, and to trust they will find the people who need them, because of the passion and dedication of librarians, booksellers, publishers, and readers.

I do want to carry over some of the acknowledgments from the original *Wide Awake* here. Thanks to Green Day, Bright Eyes, U2, Jens Lekman, Jimmy Eat World, Le Tigre, and Dar Williams for giving me fuel to write my "protest novel." Thanks to my parents, for my principles, and to my family and my family of friends. Thanks to Mr. Sachsel for teaching me about Bleeding Kansas, and Thomas Frank (in book form) and Beth Bryan and Nick Robideau (in conversation form) for teaching me about Kansas in the early 2000s. Thank you for Rachel Cohn and Rob Brittain, who were the book's earliest readers. Thank you again to the librarians who care. And thank you to everyone at Random House (in 2006 and 2024), especially my champion editor, Nancy Hinkel. There'll be time enough for rocking when we're old (we're not there yet!). In the meantime, let's make some noise.